MW01138756

On A Red Horse

This book is dedicated to Peter, James, Stephen, Jess, and all my people at the Little Amps Coffee Roasters in Harrisburg, PA.

Chapter One

Men like him were the reason aliens hadn't yet made contact with Earth. For twenty minutes Scarlet sat at a small table in The White Horse Café and watched the man prowl from one woman to another. He seemed intent on picking someone up with the focus of last call as opposed to first thing in the morning. As he struck out with lucky lady number five, his crosshairs fixed on her. He approached with a swagger and for a moment Scarlet longed for the bite of a sword hilt against her hand.

She answered before he spoke without even glancing up from the screen of the iPhone clutched between her palms. "If you plan to start this exchange with some sort of cheesy pick up line involving a piece of my anatomy, I'm going to stop you right there."

His posture stooped in her peripheral vision. "I just wanted to say that you're beautiful." His tone held a surprising note of vehemence, but he did nothing more and slinked off without another word.

The proper human emotion might be remorse for speaking to him that way, but she felt nothing as he finally left the shop. A shadow fell across her screen a moment later, and she looked up to find the café's owner and her friend, Katherine. Her friend's black hair stuck out wayward and free around her face, hanging against her neck in kinky curls. It only made the light olive of her skin stand out against the bourbon color of her eyes.

"You know you should try to be nicer to people."

Scarlet noted the tone of reproach in her voice but didn't care. "Is everyone in the building still alive?"

"Well, yes."

"Then I'm being nice."

Katherine huffed in that way that made Scarlet very aware she was in the wrong before gently tucking a strand of Scarlet's long straight brown hair behind her ear. "Cloris wants us to try harder." Katherine always mothered the group. The gentle soul hadn't yet realized she didn't need to take care of two thousand year old immortals.

Scarlet put the phone on the table with a clatter and stared up at her friend. "She asked you to speak to me, and you're trying to be nice."

Katherine's lip curled up at the corner. "So you're really not as bad at this interaction thing as you let on."

"I don't understand humans, but I understand you and the others. That's enough for me."

"If you need help or have questions...ask me. I've gotten good at this."

"It's not sex ed, Katherine. I can't just get the run down and hope for the best."

Scarlet gave her one last scowl and picked up the phone again bringing the conversation to a close. They'd spent the last three years trying to fit into the human world, and by all accounts they had succeeded. But everyone else seemed to have a niche where Scarlet really didn't fit in. She swallowed a pang of guilt as it attempted to claw up her throat from her chest. Tyr entered her mind, but she resolved not to think of him and how he'd always been the only being who ever made her feel normal. She never had to be anyone but herself. The others made her feel guilty for wanting to fight, for not wanting to give up a destiny two thousand years in the making. But where her friends went, so did she.

Katherine set a glass of espresso in front of her and disappeared behind the vast counter again without a word. Work started in an hour, and heaven knew she needed the caffeine. Her morning workout had been somewhat brutal even by her standards.

She made a note to apologize for snapping at Katherine and try to make an effort. The thought of finding a boyfriend to appease them crossed her mind every couple of months, but she didn't think a mere human could withstand her constant deluge of depression and paranoia. Scarlet tried to recall if she had always been that way or if it surfaced since they joined the human world. She stopped herself from thinking on it too hard because she honestly didn't want the answer.

As the bitter espresso coated her tongue she sighed out loud and swiped through the daily news on her CNN app. News and coffee. If humans suddenly stopped making them both, she would gladly open her seal and end the world because she'd have nothing else to live for. After a few minutes of reading, she switched to a new app moving through the world's media in small bites. It took some time, but she had learned the biases of each news station so she could try to filter it out. When she discovered the ease of which these people could ignite a war, she became entranced by the causes. The skyrocketing gas prices or a bombing in a village were just a few of an entire array of reasons and excuses to bring out her bad side. As she read each story she longed to feel the grip of her sword in her palm, the jar of metal pounding against metal. A fight, she wanted a fight, but not a person or being on this God forsaken planet could stand against her and live.

A voice interrupted. "I don't know why you watch that crap."

Scarlet glanced up to find her friend Bianca staring down at her. She gave a matching scowl to the one she'd given Katherine before Bianca kissed her on the cheek and danced out of reach. Scarlet watched her go behind the counter and tie on her apron before returning her attention to her phone.

The time passed too fast. Scarlet tossed back the rest of the espresso and grabbed her coat. The cold pressed around her as she exited the café, nearly suffocating in its bone biting intensity. She slipped her phone into her pocket and donned the cashmere-lined gloves Cloris had given her during the last holiday season. The scarf Bianca had knit for her lay forgotten in her gym bag, and now she regretted not grabbing it before leaving the house. The gloves didn't help because her hands had already taken up a dull ache. Of all the things she despised about the human world, the cold was the worst. It sucked the warmth from her body like a leech and remained unrelenting against clothing and heat sources.

Scarlet also abhorred the holiday season accompanying the cold. Had a child been born in such a magical way, why would humanity still celebrate that birth and do so with tinsel and overpriced marketing? Not to mention the fact that she'd never even seen this Almighty, and she resided in the same pantheon. But in the void they often didn't encounter any others so that really wasn't saying much.

The family part she understood. Her companions were her family, the only thing left to her in this world. She endured this torturous life for them. When Cloris suggested they leave the void, Scarlet thought it some sort of practical joke meant to discomfort them. She certainly had a strange sense of humor. As time passed, she realized her companions were unhappy in the void and remained because of her reticence. She had finally relented and followed them to Earth.

She let herself reminisce about her life before weather and rent payments, but all too soon her thoughts drifted to Tyr and she locked down the memories like a bank vault door slamming shut. She walked the rest of the way to her office building counting each step to avoid the sounds in her own head. When she arrived at work, she only wanted to leave. Scarlet entered, her heart somehow heavier.

"Good morning, Scarlet," the security guard said as she scanned her badge allowing her access to the heart of the building. She gave him her usual perfunctory nod before proceeding to the elevator and her workstation.

Her computer log-in screen glowed at her. If she didn't know it to be an inanimate object, she might have described the way it sat there leering at her as malicious. She enjoyed the fantasy of swinging a club through it. Often the delusions involved sparks, flying metal, and on very special occasions, a small fire. Instead of indulging in another deluge of the fantastical, she sat down in her swivel chair and spun to face the beast with a sneer. Once she pressed the correct combination of keys, her workload for the day popped up.

At one point she had worked the sales section and part of her job had been to cold call individuals, but that turned out to be a terrible job for her. Apparently she lacked the necessary cordial personality to sell things. Her current job required her to field help calls from users who didn't understand the basic functions of the equipment they had been duped into buying.

She scanned the list and found a few regulars. One kindly old gentleman she didn't even mind speaking to every week. He had yet to figure out how to connect to the Internet after weeks of talking to her. She began to suspect it was a ruse in order to have someone to talk with. He'd recount stories about his goldfish and the nurse who brought him meals every day. Scarlet would listen because he never asked anything of her.

As she started to dial her first help call of the day, a deep voice bellowed through the room. "Scarlet!"

She froze. Surely the voice hadn't meant her. No human alive dared raise their voice to her. After a moment of confusion, she popped her head up and looked around. A tall man towered over the workspace, definitely out of place. She ducked down so fast her knee slammed into the desk. Scarlett muttered a soft curse. Her heart shot into her throat, and she tried to swallow the fear rocketing through her. Her mind skittered to formulate a strategy. If she stayed there, he'd hunt her down to the very last cubicle. She could crawl out the side door, but more than likely he would see and find her anyway. She recognized his voice, and it promised vengeance.

"Woman, I know you're here. I can smell you. Come out," the man bellowed. She heard the menacing growl in his voice as he shuffled closer to where she hid.

Her face flamed hot. He would have no idea how much he embarrassed her at that moment. She looked down at her outfit: a sensible black pencil skirt, short black pumps, thick black stockings, and a purple cardigan. He might not even recognize her dressed like this, or wearing clothes for that matter. She wanted to ignore him, but he would look through every cubicle until he found her and wouldn't be quiet about it. After a moment she swallowed her nerves and stood up to face him. He had moved further down an aisle but caught sight of her as soon as she showed herself.

"I finally found you, woman," he shouted with a lopsided smile and stalked toward her. The closer he got the higher she had to trail her gaze up or risk being reminded of better times. He was barely dressed, save a few pieces of leather and some fur. *The man descended on the NYC streets in the dead of winter like that?* Certainly not the craziest she'd seen people dress around town though. Once he made it to her, she pulled him into her cubicle by his good left arm and shoved him into the open seat across from her, away from her nosy coworkers' eyes.

He smiled at the close quarters and reached out to her, but she pushed him away so the chair sat against the opposite wall of her workspace.

"What are you doing here?"

"Looking for you," he said as if the answer was obvious. His forehead scrunched in the cutest way, but the softness that action inspired withered as his eyes roamed down her body.

His leer was the least of her concerns as she looked at his leather pants and animal fur stole. "And what are you wearing?"

"What I always wear. And is that how you greet your husband after so long an absence?"

"What were you expecting?" she asked, squinting at his furs. "Does that animal even exist on Earth?"

"A kiss perhaps, and of course it's a—"he broke off to lift the face of the beast to his"—it's a fox." He didn't sound very confident in that assessment.

The truth: once upon a time they shared more than one passionate embrace. The memories of the last time he had cupped her face and kissed her lips surged forward as if by their own volition. But that Scarlet and the current Scarlet were two different beings, so she pushed the images away. The mortal world broke her like nothing else in existence had even come close to before. All Tyr would do here was corrupt the life of simplicity she had painstakingly created to preserve any remaining parts of herself.

"I will not kiss you, Tyr. I no longer know you. Nor myself for that matter."

He lifted her chin gently with his one huge hand and forced her to meet his eyes. The god of justice had an intense gaze with emerald eyes that seemed to burn through one's soul making it impossible to keep a secret if he wanted the answer.

"What has become of you, my love? Why do you hide your eyes from mine?"

"Why are you here, Tyr? It's been three years."

"Aye, and I have been searching heaven and hell to find you during that time. I finally went to the All Father—my father—and asked his guidance. On his advice I found you here."

Great, now the All Father knew where to find me. Not that any sort of subterfuge mattered with him.

"I'll say it again, go home. There is nothing for you here."

At first he didn't respond only forced her to hold his gaze. He gripped her face a little tighter, and she scowled at him before wrenching away. Tyr knew better than to touch her like that.

The look on his face said she had proved a point he wanted desperately to make. "You would have ripped off my hand and fed it to me had I touched you like that three years ago."

"No, I wouldn't have. I would hate to deprive you of your love life."

"Very clever."

A squat man who looked distinctly gray, both in appearance and personality, stuck his head into her cubicle looked at both of them for a second before scuttling away. Both immortals stared after the man, but Scarlet recovered first. "That was my boss; you need to leave."

He sat back as if he might get more comfortable squeezed into a small bit of metal and plastic. "War answers to no man."

"Except you, you mean."

"You said it."

"Say goodbye and leave," she warned, her anger simmering now. As much as this reminder of home was comforting, she still had no intention of going anywhere with him, even if he begged. The image of him nude doing just that clouded her mind for a moment, and she pushed it away. But for one fleeting second a fire entered her blood. A jolt of exhilaration she hadn't felt in years. Damn, it felt good.

"Goodbye and leave?" he repeated, dragging her from her reminiscence.

"Just go."

"I will not. Not until you agree to see me later."

"No."

"Then I won't leave."

"You're going to cost me my job."

"You don't need to be working. I'm your husband and I'm meant to take care of you."

"Yeah, if this was 1900 and I was some random human chick looking to simply become a homemaker and create babies," she shot back.

He reached out and gripped her hand reverently before placing a kiss on the back of it. Her center melted from the inside out, as it always did when he kissed her.

"Even after all this time there is something between us. I feel it, and I know you do too."

She wanted to deny it, to push him away, but there had always been that connection between them, even from the moment they'd met. In his presence her heart speed up and her palms grew sweaty. He touched something inside her she couldn't deny. Denying it would be as bad as depriving herself of oxygen or food, in other words, unnatural.

She recalled how she had made him feel self-conscious about his hand and the nickname given to him by the All Father's children. She agreed to a bet with him that night. He'd claimed he could give her more pleasure with one hand than any man with two. She didn't know, even to this day, why she took that bet, but it changed her life and his. Her skin grew hot thinking about the night they'd spent together. She tried to duck her head so he couldn't see the tell-tale pink tracking up her neck and into her cheeks.

"If I agree to see you later, will you please go? And also buy real clothes. People don't dress like that here. Or anywhere for that matter."

"If you give me a place and time, I'll make the agreement."

She scribbled her gym address on a yellow sticky-note and shoved it at his chest. "Be there at five thirty; we can talk then. You better be dressed properly."

He kissed her hand and left the cubicle. All she could do was drop her head onto the edge of her desk and hope she was still employed.

What if she had stayed with him? She couldn't fathom others being given the mantles her and her companions wore for the past few thousand years. Nor did she think Cloris would even allow another take that position. If she had stayed in the void maybe the destiny they'd shared would have just slipped away, unknown, and never come to pass...or maybe something worse.

Scarlet didn't want to dwell on it. For now this was her life, her job, and that squat little man was her boss. She scooted toward the desk and picked up her headset determined to finish the day without another interruption to her routine.

Chapter Two

Tyr sauntered from the metal tower amidst the stares of human men and women alike. It didn't matter though because he finally found Scarlet, and he wouldn't be letting her go anytime soon. The men he saw were sad, little humans. The women could never compare to his woman, so they were also beneath his notice. She asked him to find appropriate clothing, and so he would.

He walked down the street to a store he knew to be a popular place amongst the mortal men. A woman approached him as he entered, and he sized her up. She wasn't as tall or in as good physical condition as his bride, but perhaps she knew men's clothing well.

"My wife asked me to wear appropriate clothing," he told the woman as she appraised him from the top of his head to the tips of his boots. At six feet four inches he towered almost an entire foot over her, so she tilted her head back in order to see all of him.

"I can certainly help you with that, sir. Right this way."

She led him to a dressing room behind a fogged glass window and took less than a minute to measure him completely. For a human she was impressive.

"Just one moment, sir, and I'll bring a few things for you to try."

She left and returned with a suit and a coat. The woman eyed his missing right hand while kneeling to take his boots away for leather shoes, but he politely declined them. Those boots were made from the hides of wolves he'd hunted before this woman's family had begun to spread across the Earth. They were almost as precious to him as his wife, not that this little human could understand such things.

He put on the suit and let her take away the leathers. While he stood in front of the mirror, he decided he couldn't dress well and not do something about his hair.

When she returned he asked, "Do you have something I can use for my hair?"

She looked around before a light entered her eyes, and she pulled an elastic from her own wrist. It smelled of her, but Tyr didn't mind. Once in his hair, he wouldn't notice. She watched rapt as he quickly braided his shoulder length hair and secured the end with the brown elastic that blended into his own chestnut colored hair.

The attendant nodded her approval. "Looks good."

Tyr now looked almost like every other man on the street, save his height and weeks of beard growth. He would have shaved if he'd actually thought he would find Scarlet today. She eluded him for so long he doubted he would ever find her, but he had kept looking.

He hadn't been exaggerating when he said he searched heaven and hell for her. The shining realm was a quick check because she would have stood out in a place like that. The Underworld took longer, mainly because its occupying goddess, Hel, had been reluctant to allow him to leave. She'd claimed it had been millennia since a man had entered her bed and practically begged him to stay. Had he been a minor deity, he might have been captured whether he'd wished to join her or not.

The memory of the stench of her breath and her complete lack of sex appeal reminded him of the sulfur stricken realm. He curled his lip before shaking away the memory. He hated stepping foot in the Underworld, but for Scarlet he would endure anything, including Hel's disgusting advances. Maybe if the goddess bathed once in a while she might not be so lonely.

The sales woman reminded him of her presence as she stroked his upper arm under the guise of checking the material.

"I'm ready to pay now." He handed the sales girl a plastic card Thor had given him upon leaving Asgard, and she took it away.

After concluding the business at the shop, he had no other errand save going to the location where Scarlet asked him to meet her. Back on the street he searched for a clock on one of the many-screened surfaces in New York City. Six hours remained. A yellow conveyance pulled up, and he directed the driver to the gym address Scarlet gave him. Once he arrived he sat on a bench outside to wait. The humans had long been a point of fascination to him, rather like ants in a glass house. He could watch them flitter this way and that as they went about their lives. While they looked harmless and innocuous, they could turn from victim to predator at the slightest provocation. Even something that would seem of little consequence to one of them could set another off enough to do fatal damage.

He'd witnessed it over and over, and yet it still held him in sway. That particular human aspect made him all the more curious as to why Scarlet would choose to live among them. She disliked the human world even more than most immortals. As he'd searched for her, he realized it was likely her friends' decision to leave the void. He admired Scarlet's loyalty to her friends. Well, before she left him for them.

He recalled the moment as if it happened the day before. He woke and found her no longer at his side. Her absence burned like a void in his soul. He vowed from that day he would not rest until he found her. The other gods mocked him, but he found their behavior no different than any other day. The hours passed in a blur as he watched the humans, men, women, and their offspring, pass him by. He felt Scarlet's presence like a brush of warm fragrant air the moment she walked up the street.

His eyes met hers as if by force, and he swallowed the desire to run to her and wrap his arms around her lean frame. When she finally made it to him, he smiled up at her from his seat on the bench. "My love, thank you of keeping your word."

"When have I not?"

His smile slipped as his heart hardened a little. "Until death do us part, I believe."

She pursed her lips but said nothing as she pressed forward. "This is not a date. I come here to work out every day, and you wanted to talk. So I figured we could do that while I work out."

"Have I dressed appropriately for you?"

"A little over-dressed, but a huge improvement over that fox—"she gestured to his neck area"—thing."

He bowed his head at the compliment and stood to follow her into the gym. Now that he thought about it the suit sales woman seemed a little taken aback by his animal skins as well. Maybe it wasn't an animal found on Earth. They moved to the back of the gym past human stares, until they reached an empty room lined with red vinyl pads and mirrors.

"Is this a sparring room?" he asked peering around and finding a light switch.

"It is. You're the only being in my vicinity who can withstand me in a sparring match, and I need to burn off some energy."

He shrugged out of his jacket. "It would be my pleasure."

Tyr smiled broadly as she stripped her own clothing and put on shorts and a sports bra with her back turned. Something he'd witnessed her doing countless times, and yet it never held any less awe for him. She'd toned up even more than the last time he had the opportunity to see her nude, and she looked good enough to bite. Even now he wanted to sink his teeth into the small hollow at her hipbone.

"Stop staring," she said as she plopped to the mats to stretch. He stood and watched her maneuver from one position to the other with absolutely no acknowledgment of the effect she had on him. He wanted nothing more than to push her back to the mats and show her why she wanted him to begin with. But after three years, he did not want to scare her away. He swallowed the lump in his throat but dared not remove his gaze from her.

"Are you ready?" she asked finally, standing and bouncing back and forth on her bare feet.

"Of course."

She shook her head and approached to reach up to loosen the silk necktie. He had become so wound up in watching Scarlet he forgot the thing the sales woman chose to match his eyes.

After a moment he met her gaze, but instead of love or even her cold aloofness of the morning, he stood before War. He had done something in error, and she was about to make him pay for it. "What is it?"

"You come to New York to find me and then come here smelling of another woman?"

He rolled his eyes forgetting with whom he was dealing with for a second. "You misunderstand. The woman who sold me this suit gave me something for which to secure my hair."

She reached behind his head and pulled the elastic out roughly before tossing it away. "You will never smell of another woman when you come to me again."

He smirked. "You're going to allow an *again*?

Tyr crossed the line, and she was on edge. He was flat on his back, the mat cushioning him before he even realized what had happened. She sat on his chest with her knees almost up into his armpits.

"You have improved, I see," he quipped, reaching up to cup her left hip.

"I was always a little gentle on you. Pity, I guess." She sneered yanking his hand away and pinning it up by his head. She had gone too far over his boundaries now.

He pinned her right knee with this forearm and rolled her over taking a dominant position, until she wrapped her thighs around his waist and locked her feet behind his back. He scooted forward so her knees were almost perpendicular to her head, and she relented. He tossed her over to the side and pinned her so he could look into her eyes while pressing his weight across her body.

"You will never pity me. You did that very first day, and I showed you how wrong you were for doing so. Do I need to show you again?"

He had touched something there. A hard glint entered her eyes, and she pursed her lips, almost in invitation for a kiss. He wanted to take it so much that he flexed his hand into the mat to establish a grounding point.

"Release me," she said through gritted teeth. He did so at once and sat back on his feet still crouched to the mats. She stood, walked over to a mirror, and looked down at her feet.

This was a new development. No matter how far she pushed him and how much he hated her sometimes; she was his woman. *Until death do us part* was the vow they'd taken and he would make her see he took that seriously. Regardless, he cared for her well-being. "Are you well, my love?"

"I'm fine, and stop calling me that." She turned to face him. "We need to get a divorce."

The words hit him like a punch to the stomach. Each inhale and exhale became physically painful as he met her eyes. They were red-rimmed and almost misty as if she might cry, but he knew better than that. This woman had no heart. She did not do something as pitiable as weep. He steeled his heart and put on a mask of arrogance, one he'd perfected long ago to endure the emotional torment at the hands of his so-called family. Even she would be unable to see through it.

Chapter Three

The words climbed out of her throat on a wave of nausea and hung in the air between them creating a heavy tension. Scarlet looked away, like a coward, so she couldn't see his face. He always had such an expressive face, and she couldn't stand to see the heartbreak in those beautiful eyes.

She heard him speaking but couldn't make out his words over the sound of her heart pounding in her ears. Tears pooled at the corner of her eyes, but she wouldn't allow them to fall. She would burn the Earth to ash before anyone saw her cry. Finally his words broke through the sound of her own heartbeat.

"My love, I said, 'until death do us part.' Unless you're prepared to kill me here and now, then you will not get what you desire."

She swung around to face him. He wore a look of pure arrogance and dare she say it, challenge. He wasn't listening or taking her seriously.

"In case you didn't notice I live on Earth now, not in the void and not in Asgard. Here. I have a very different life than the one I had before and in that life there is no—"she gestured between the two of them"—us."

One corner of his mouth turned up, and he stalked closer reaching for her. She backed up until her shoulder blades hit the cool glass of the mirror. "These humans have broken you. You retreat. War does not retreat."

She swallowed and looked down at her hands. His words were true no matter how much it pained her to hear them. He didn't stop but continued forward until his body stood flush with hers. She looked up into his eyes and forgot what they were fighting about. She saw her happiness there, the nights spent in each other's embrace, and more specifically how often and passionately they'd made love. The walls in his home in Asgard had shaken with the sound of their lovemaking.

He leaned down so inches separated their lips, but she could not look away from his eyes. Tyr cupped her face moving closer centimeter by centimeter, slowly torturing her with anticipation. She could have pushed forward and closed the distance between them, or she could have smacked her head on the mirror behind her to get away from the inevitable. Hell, she might have even been able to toss him to the ground and scurry away. The problem was...he was absolutely correct. War did not back down, especially to invading Norse gods with kissable lips.

When his lips finally touched hers it felt as though she had stood there for a lifetime waiting for it. The taste of him foreign and yet so familiar. As if they hadn't stopped kissing each other, not for a single day. He growled into her mouth as his hand trailed to the back of her neck and his fingers slid into her hair. She followed suit reaching up to clutch the expensive fabric of his shirt to pull him closer.

Scarlet pressed into his lips harder until he opened and she could entwine her tongue with his. He tasted like sunshine and the ozone that permeates the air just before a thunderstorm. His beard rubbed her chin and around her mouth. It had grown past the stubble phase, but she didn't mind the additional sensation it brought to the moment.

His hand tightened in her hair as he delved deeper into her mouth, pulling her as much as she was him. The hard press of his erection growing between them snapped her out of a lust induced haze. One second they were kissing and the next she had pushed him to the floor. Scarlet stood with her back pressed against the mirror, her hands leaving warm fogging prints against the clean glass.

"Woman," he warned in a low a growl.

Anyone else might have cowered at that tone, but she reveled in it. Loved it since the first time he'd made love to her and passionately whispered her name in that same gravelly voice. Every part of her body and heart wanted to mount him right there on the floor and make up for the three years they'd lost, but her head told her no. It reminded her of the nights she'd spent alone in her bed, and warned her of when he would tire of the human world and return to Asgard, as he most certainly would. He would leave her even more in love with him. Leave her needing him more than she had over the last three years. She didn't know if she could survive that. Ultimately the one thing that could bring down War was love.

When he pushed himself up and stared at her, she couldn't meet his eyes. "Woman, if I have to stay on this gods forsaken planet for eternity I'll take that look from your eyes."

She cleared her throat and shook herself sliding the mask of indifference she wore well into place. "What look is that?"

"The look that says you're a wounded animal. The look that does not challenge me back and say you will always win. What the hell happened that made you into this sort of woman? You're nothing like the person I fell in love with."

His words carved themselves into her heart and soul. They wounded her deeply. The bite of tears at the corner of her eyes caught her off guard, but she refused to let them fall. She couldn't remember when she had transformed from a supportive friend staying on Earth for unity to a pitiful excuse of pseudo-immortality. The word *person* had popped into her mind first, but she really wasn't. She needed to keep reminding herself of that fact. It seemed every time she let herself get comfortable something showed up to remind her who she was and wasn't.

Scarlet slid down the mirror to the ground and put her head in her hands. "I don't know. I don't know."

Tyr scooted over until his back touched the mirror beside her and gathered her into his arms so she could lean on his shoulder. She wouldn't cry, but she would allow him to comfort her for a few minutes. Just a few minutes.

"I thought we were going to spar?" he asked after a few moments of blessed, comfortable silence.

"We were, but I feel like yelling at you has helped."

He inhaled deeply, and she forced herself to meet his eyes. "Was I not enough for you?" he asked.

With a few words he broke her heart all over again. If she told him the truth, it would give him hope. If she lied, it would break her a little more, cracking the fragile shell her soul had become without him. Minutes passed as he waited for her answer. She may not let her tears fall, but she could clearly see a pool of them building in his eyes. Deep enough that he looked away. She couldn't lie. "You have always been enough for me."

He pulled away from her, breaking all contact. "You pity me, just as everyone else does."

"What about you is there to pity? You're beautiful, kind, just, and the sexiest being I have ever come across. Hades not included."

Tyr turned to glare at her. "Has that bastard touched you?"

She laughed at the absurdity. Hades hadn't touched anyone or anything, including himself, for over two millennia. "No, but the man is beautiful and not a soul living or dead can refute it."

He nodded. The trust he had for her even after she'd left him, after she'd accused him of sleeping around on the day he'd returned, and after almost bedding him in her gym astounded her. "If you will not come back with me, I'll stay here with you."

"You can't stay here. The prophecy is one thing to consider and then there is the fact that after some time you will begin stepping on humans just to be rid of them."

"I could not step on them. I am not that tall."

"I was being a smart ass."

"And the prophecy is of little consequence. I went to the Underworld and nothing happened. Not a hellhound in sight."

"You went to the Underworld!" She jumped up and turned away in an attempt to burn some of the fire that shot through her. He went to the Underworld. *The man went to the Underworld.* What person in his right mind went there of his own free will? "You're prophesied to be killed by a hellhound. Why would you go there?"

"To find you."

"Why would I go to the Underworld?"

"I thought maybe to get away because you figured I would not follow you there."

"What made you think I didn't want to be with you?"

"How about the waking up in our bed, in our home, alone? And the three year absence that followed."

"You're an idiot. Please promise me you won't go there again."

"Only if you promise you will not make me leave and shut me out of your life again."

A draw. The very thing she'd feared when he came there. He asked the only thing she had vowed she wouldn't give him when she left work. She'd barely got any work done at all between her coworkers constant gossip about the events that took place and the fact that she could think of nothing but Tyr. After he'd left, she considered taking a leave of absence, but that would be doing the opposite of keeping her life on track. No, she would press on, business as usual, until Tyr left.

"You can stay with me. We can figure this out." More words spoken she would likely regret. She really needed to learn to think things through before she spoke.

"Are we sparring or not?" He stood up.

"I don't feel like it anymore. I need a cold shower."

"Why?"

"You haven't taken a cold shower in the last three years?" Scarlet stopped speaking. She didn't want to know what he'd done or not done since she left. It wasn't her business who he spent his time with once she'd given him up.

"Why would I want to cascade myself with chilled water?"

She shook her head. "It's something I learned here actually. When I feel the need to have sex but not the desire to satiate myself or find a partner, I take a cold shower."

A chill entered the room and gooseflesh broke out on her arms. He rarely showed any magical ability even while living in Asgard. To do so now showed an extreme lack of control. "And how many bed partners have you had since you left me?"

"None, okay. Hence the cold shower."

He stared at her before nodding weighing her words, no doubt for truth. Yet another of his abilities.

"And you," she demanded, "how many women have had the pleasure of your bed since I have been gone?"

He had the gall to look affronted. "If you must know, none. Not that there were no offers. That is when I went in search of you. I could not stand their pity for my disability before and even more so because my woman left me."

The man always had a way of making her feel terrible. Especially when he was in the right. *Justice indeed.* "I didn't mean to cause you heartache. I honestly should have said something. I didn't exactly want to leave, but you know even with all of us out of the void it is still our charge to protect the seals. We can only do that together, where our powers are strongest."

Tyr continued on his soapbox now that he was up there. "And do the others punish themselves as you do? Do the others hold a job with a boss to command them?"

Scarlet sighed, "Well Katherine owns a café downtown, Bianca works with Katherine, and Cloris still holds her duties as Death. She couldn't really let people stop dying."

"And Hades?" he prompted.

"We don't see him that often. Usually only when Cloris commands his presence. So I have seen him maybe five times in the last three years. I think he started his own business as well, but again, I don't know much about it."

Tyr shook his head and clenched his fist against his knee. "Even now, when you gave up everything for your companions, they shut you out."

"It's not them who shut me out. I shut myself out to keep them from seeing how unhappy I am here." Another sentence spoken before proper thought. Thinking it and admitting it out loud were two different things. "I'm unhappy," she said again. "I'm unhappy."

Saying it sucked the rest of her remaining energy as if they held all the anguish she'd suffered for the last three years, or maybe that was Tyr. Either way, she liked not being alone and not feeling like a manic-depressive with anger issues. Well, the anger issues would stay, no helping that.

The thought flitted into her mind, and she couldn't stop it from blooming once it planted. Could Tyr still love her after everything she'd put him though? Or was this some sort of revenge scheme to pay her back for three years of torture. And which did she hope was the truth?

Chapter Four

Tyr was certain they'd made some progress. She wasn't making him leave, but she also wasn't inviting him back into her life. It was a start. Her admission of her own unhappiness would help his cause in the end. They donned their clothes respectively and left the gym, under the heavy stares of the rest of the gym patrons. No doubt the desk staff saw what happened between them in the sparring room, not that he minded. He wanted the entire world to know she belonged to him.

"Come on. I'll take you to a hotel," she said, pulling him toward the curb to hail a cab.

He disengaged his arm and shook his head. "No, I go with you."

"My apartment is barely large enough to fit me and the few meager possessions I have let alone another person almost twice my size."

Tyr skimmed his hand down the front of his suit jacket. "I am not twice your size."

Her mouth tipped in a tiny grin, and he realized she was teasing him. "Fine, Siren, treat me that way. I will get my revenge."

"Bring it, Justice."

Hearing her refer to him by the nickname she'd given him on the first night they'd met warmed his heart. He rubbed his suit coat on the outside right over his heart as if it might dull the ache there.

The cab pulled up, and they climbed inside. Overall it was a short trip to her apartment, and barely five minutes after getting into the taxi, they got out. The conveyance made him doubt his immortality, but that was a moral dilemma for another day.

Once they stepped onto the curb a man in a trench coat approached them, and Scarlet froze. The rigidness of her posture put Tyr on alert as he turned to face the man. That's when he noticed the smell of brimstone. He swallowed to ensure his voice didn't break when he spoke. "What do you want, hellhound?"

The man's mouth spread into a feral grin, a smile of half-madness, before he spoke in a thick, gravelly voice. "Hel requests your presence."

Scarlet stepped in front of Tyr. "He's not going anywhere."

Tyr gently put his hand on her arm but addressed the hellhound. "She is right. I concluded my business with Hel months ago. I have no business in the under realms."

The hellhound tilted his head and leaned forward as if trying to catch their scent. "If you don't come with me now, I'll shift and tear out the throat of every human I come across. Do you want your precious human life upset so much?"

He didn't doubt if Scarlet had her sword she would have cut the dog's head clean off in the middle of the street.

"Fine," Scarlet said. "But she better have a damn good reason for requesting our presence, or I'll kill her. Goddess or not, human life or not, I'm still War embodied and all that entails."

Tyr swallowed. He heard the conviction in her voice and knew she would do exactly that. Scarlet had never given him cause to fear her, but sometimes he feared for others in her wake.

The dog turned around and headed down an alley to a small open door toward the back. They descended into a basement, and when darkness enclosed them completely, they heard him snap his fingers. Suddenly they stood before the gates of the Underworld. The great, gleaming black gates opened as they approached. He wondered if they could bar those Hel didn't want to gain entry as well.

The boat sat waiting, a long boat with rows of seats. There were no oarsmen, just a withered old man in a hood and cape at the head of the boat. They climbed in but didn't move until Tyr remembered something. He stood to place two gold coins in the wrinkled, outstretched hand of their host.

As they crossed the River Styxx toward the palace beyond, Tyr watched the murky water wondering what kind of spirit or beast could live there. He couldn't see any shadows moving below the surface, but with that much water, how could it be empty? Tyr already saw many of the wonders of the Underworld during his last visit. He didn't need to do any sightseeing, but Scarlet looked out over the landscape, no doubt trying to formulate an exit strategy.

The palace loomed ahead as if it were meant for a fairy tale, the original twisted stories, not the fluffy ones with blundering princesses and charming princes. The walls were made of onyx, as were the steps that led inside. The main floors looked to be black marble with light veins throughout. Tyr would have to ask Hades how he'd built such a spectacular dwelling the next time he saw him.

When they finally reached the throne room, a throne that had once belonged to Hades, they stopped. Hel was an oddly tall woman with a too long face that showed her age more than most deities. She wore long, flowing robes of gauzy white that did nothing for her figure except accentuate the length of her torso and arms. He could see the blush of her nipples through the fabric, a sight he dearly wanted to forget. The hellhound that sat at her feet was another he recognized well, although he hadn't seen him once on his previous sojourn to the Underworld

"What do you want, Hel?" Scarlet asked taking the lead. At least she took his focus off Hel's body.

"Oh, my dear, you did not bring your sword with you. I would have so loved to see such a relic," Hel said, a mocking tone of reproach in her voice.

"My sword is gone as I no longer hold the position of Horseman."

"You have abdicated your position, and yet you still claim to be War?"

Scarlet looked confused, and Tyr grabbed her hand to keep her calm.

"How do you...?" Scarlet began but the other woman cut in.

"I hear everything my hounds hear."

The hellhound that accompanied them sat at her feet in his true form. The situation made Tyr uneasy, but he showed no fear. Hel was the kind of woman who would take advantage of any weakness.

"I'm War. Regardless of where I live, or if I carry the sword, I still have the power to turn men upon one another and take peace from the Earth. That is who I am, and it will not change until the prophecy gains enough power to call upon four new Horsemen."

"What else is within your power, child?" She held up her hand to stop them. "Wait, what is the prophecy? Let me see if I get it right," she said to herself more than them. *"When He broke the second seal, I heard the second living creature saying, 'Come and see.' And another, a red horse, went out; and to him who sat on it, it was granted to take peace from the earth, and that men would slay one another; and a great sword was given to him."*

They all knew the prophecy, and they knew *she* knew the prophecy. Scarlet grew visibly impatient with Hel. He saw it in the flex of her fingers and the set of her shoulders.

"Why are you so curious? What do you want with me, and what do you want with Tyr? I don't like games."

Hel's eyes shifted to Tyr for the first time. "My darling, how good of you to come back to me. I so missed you when you left."

He tightened his grip on Scarlet's hand, and she returned it. "I did not have a choice, it would seem."

"You look so delectable too. Will you not stay here once your friend goes home?"

"She is not my friend nor my lover nor my acquaintance. As I told you before, she is my wife."

"And yet, she left you. I feel that says something."

"We have since renewed our relationship, and under the eyes of all the realms she is my wife still."

Hel opened her mouth to speak again, but Scarlet interrupted. "What do you want Hel? We don't have all day to stand here. I'm tired. If we are going to fight, get on with it."

Hel rose from her black throne. *No, Hades' black throne*, Tyr reminded himself as they watched her descend. She was almost as tall as Tyr and almost as masculine.

"I know how unhappy you are in the human world," she said to Scarlet. "I know you wish for a different life. I'm here to offer it to you in exchange for something I want."

"And what is that?"

"Hades."

Scarlet burst into laughter. Completely uncharacteristic of her. "You think I command Hades? You're insane."

Hel continued to smile, and Tyr grew more uncomfortable. "I know you don't control Hades, but you have influence with his keeper, Death." Hel said the name in a growl, and wind ripped through the palace tearing at their hair and clothing. "Besides, if they knew of your marriage and how you left the man you love so they could be happy, they will feel indebted to you. You would simply need to ask for what you want."

"Not what I want, what you want. And while Hades follows Cloris, he does not take orders from anyone, especially her. I don't think they even speak."

"Then perhaps he would welcome the opportunity to come home."

Tyr tried to recall the last time he laid eyes on Hades. He barely saw the man in the void while the group lived there but definitely crossed paths with him. Hades wasn't easily forgettable. So beautiful he was unable to show his true form to humans, so lovely every goddess, immortal, and semi-deity threw themselves at his feet. There was a time Tyr wanted such things, to be a whole man and have goddesses lining up to enter his bed. When he thought about it, he pitied Hades.

Scarlet spoke again. "I don't know what he wants or doesn't want. I have spoken to him five times tops in the last three years. I'll relay your message."

Scarlet turned to go but the hellhound jumped down and circled her with a growl. She gave it the look of death and crouched before it. "With one touch I can make your friends your enemies. With one touch I can make you turn on your own pack, your own goddess. Get out of my way, dog."

She straightened and walked toward the door before turning back and leveling Tyr with a cold stare. He glanced down at the dog who moved back to Hel's side and then followed Scarlet from the chamber. They were ferried back across the river and then exited the same alleyway they'd come, finding themselves back on the busy New York City streets.

Scarlet took a deep breath of city air, fresher than the stench of the Underworld, as she stood in the middle of the sidewalk. "I have to see the others, and I'm going to have to tell them about you."

"Good. Maybe they will show you the error of your ways."

"I'm not in the mood right now, Tyr," she said digging a phone from her jacket and quickly pressing keys. After a few moments, she hailed a cab, and they both climbed in.

They proceeded uptown to a brownstone with a festive front porch. Tyr looked around for more hellhounds as they climbed the steps. Scarlet rang the bell, and they entered to the sound of a small, yapping animal. He almost stepped on the beast as he entered, but it had apparently become adept at not getting trampled.

He followed Scarlet into a sitting area. Two gray couches sat against the outer walls and bookshelves lined the wall across from the windows. Tyr wanted to look at the titles, but Scarlet's look had him turning toward the assembled collective. He had only seen the group together a few times and never really spoke to them. He only visited the void out of necessity and then only to see Scarlet when she requested his presence. They married in Asgard with his family present.

"Everyone," Scarlet said and then gestured toward Tyr. "This is my husband."

He raised his hand and waved, unsure of what to say.

"You have one hand." A small girl who looked no more than seventeen said from the end of the couch. She had her legs drawn up to her chest and her big, round eyes fixed on him. He couldn't be sure which of the horsemen she was.

"Tyr, Bianca. Bianca, Tyr."

He gave her a regal nod and turned toward the others. Death he recognized as she traveled all the realms. Hades he also recognized, leaving Katherine. She was the motherly one of the group, but he'd heard nasty rumors that she harbored a much darker side. Her dark brown, curly hair was held atop her head by some sticks, and as she surveyed him he almost thought he saw her eyes shift. After a moment, he shook it off, gave her a similar nod, and looked away.

He took a seat near Hades. He didn't particularly want to sit near the man, but to be honest it was probably the safest place in the room.

"So when exactly did you get married?" Bianca asked.

"Tyr and I were married a little while before we decided to leave the void."

"You did not think to tell us?" Cloris said, her voice low and seductive, even though she most certainly didn't look like she meant it to be.

"It wasn't relevant," Scarlet said. "You all decided we were leaving. I had no choice but to follow. Even if we don't reside in the void, the seals are still our responsibility, and we can only protect them together."

Death cast her glance toward Hades who locked his jaw and refused to meet her gaze. Tyr would have bet good gold that something happened or was happening between those two. It would seem natural. Death and the god of the Underworld.

"But none of this is why we are here," Scarlet said, pacing a few steps before stopping to remove her high heels and then resuming again.

"Hel commanded our presence in the Underworld, and I believe she means to bring on the Apocalypse."

Chapter Five

Everyone jumped up at once, except Tyr who remained sitting with his hand resting on his knee. The man knew how to keep a cool head about him. That had always been such an attractive feature.

"Just wait," Scarlet said. "Everyone sit, and I'll explain what happened."

She recounted how Tyr hunted for her, then the encounter with the hellhound, and finally her threat and their exit.

Hades spoke first, and it almost hurt her to listen to him speak. "Hel wants me in her bed again." He spoke softly with a feminine cadence, but his voice was richer, more melodious as if it were meant to entrance and ensnare. Some even said it sounded different for each person who heard it.

"It would seem she wants him desperately if she all but abducted a horsemen to question on the matter," Cloris said side-eyeing Hades.

Scarlet glanced back and forth between them. "Did I miss something?"

"No." Death's reply was terse and final.

Scarlet paced back and forth shaking her hands. They always tingled when her adrenaline spiked. "I told her nothing save what would happen if she threatened me again."

"Can we get back to this husband?" Bianca asked eyeing Tyr.

Scarlet stopped pacing and glared at her. "We have a crisis situation here, and you want to know about my husband?"

She stood and crossed the room to look at him. "Of course. He is part of the family now."

Scarlet watched as Tyr shifted in his seat, uncertain of what he was supposed to do when confronted by Bianca.

"Give me your hand," Bianca said as she reached out.

He didn't hesitate and offered it to her palm up. She cupped his big hand in both of her small ones and stared into the center of his palm.

"You're a brave one and true. Just for the sake of being just not because you enjoy the recognition that might come from it. You have claimed Scarlet completely as your own, and you offer yourself to her with no conditions."

Tyr met Scarlet's eyes as Bianca read his palm, and she forced herself to hold his gaze. Bianca took up palm reading about a thousand years ago. She had grown eerily good at it in that time.

After a moment longer she let his hand go and patted his cheek before crossing back to her own spot, tucking her knees up, and resting her chin on them.

"Did you see anything else?" Tyr asked.

"Of course," Bianca replied, but she did not elaborate or share what else she might have seen.

It didn't matter. Bianca approved him being there, and that was enough for the others. One by one, starting with Katherine, they crossed to him and kissed him gently on the cheek welcoming him to the family in their own way. Hades didn't approach or even look at him for that matter, but Tyr didn't seem to mind. When they finished, Scarlet stood staring at them.

"Guys. He's not staying."

Bianca snorted and smiled a secret-keeping smile.

"I stay," Tyr said. "I'll stay by your side until the last breath is gone from my body. This I vow."

"Witnessed," Death said.

Scarlet shook her head and sank down onto the carpet as if she were on a carnival ride she wasn't allowed to dismount. "I don't have a choice in this. Do I?" she whispered in defeat a few moments later.

"It would seem not, love," Bianca said.

"Fine. You stay. But I'm going to find a new place to live. He will have to duck through every doorway in my building."

"I don't mind," Tyr said after a moment.

"You should quit your job too," Bianca said. "Come work at the Café. You will be so much happier."

Scarlet pursed her lips and sighed with exaggerated force. "Is that a suggestion, Bianca, or did you see it?"

The girl shrugged and put her head back on her knees. Bianca often didn't reveal some of the things she saw. She said there was a natural order to things, and sometimes people needed to reach conclusions and solutions on their own. Supernatural help was well and good, but she didn't believe in just dishing it out willy-nilly. Scarlet often saw her read the less fortunate and help in any way she could, like sending a young pregnant woman off with her tips for the day telling her to buy a red scarf or small things like that.

"Now, the question remains," Death said breaking the heavy silence. "Would Hel really end the world just to get Hades?"

Not a few seconds passed before Tyr, Hades, and Scarlet spoke in unison. "Yes."

Death pressed on. "Well then. Do you think she knows the parameters of the seals?"

Bianca shook her head slowly looking off into the distance. "No, but I think she has her suspicions about some of them."

"She did ask after my sword," Scarlet said.

"Which hellhound did she have with her?" Hades asked barely above a whisper.

"She sent another hellhound to fetch us, but it was Garmr who sat at her right hand," Tyr growled.

They all looked at him. "Do you know him?" Death asked.

"We have a prophecy."

"What sort of prophecy?" Bianca asked.

"I'm to play a role at Ragnarok. The prophecy says, 'Then shall the dog, Garmr, be loosed, which is bound before Gnipahellir: he is the greatest monster; he shall do battle with Tyr, and each become the other's slayer.'"

Death looked at him and tilted her head to the side. "You have a death prophecy then. These things can change in time."

"It has not since the Ragnarok was foretold, and I no longer question it."

"Wasn't it weird seeing him then?" Bianca asked. Her interest in Tyr was strange and definitely out of character. Scarlet wondered if something in a vision caught her attention or if she was simply curious about the new addition to the group.

"No." He shook his head. "We shall become each other's slayer at the end of days. Hopefully that will not be soon, and until then I do not worry over things I cannot control."

"Amen, man." Bianca said with an appreciative nod.

Hades interrupted the banter and looked between Scarlet and Tyr. "Did she sit on the black throne?"

"She did. Does that matter?" Scarlet asked.

"No," Hades shook his head ever so slightly sending his brown ringlets spinning perfectly. "It only matters to me." He glanced back at Death and fell silent.

Scarlet often feared there was more to Hades' life before he began his service with them than he let on. When Hades came to them after their first creation, they knew Hel had already taken control of the Underworld and that Hades had been captured as her war prize. Unfortunately, even gods sometimes can't help their own outcomes, and he remained under her *care* until he joined The Horsemen.

He seemed scarred by that experience, and in the few moments she'd spent in Hel's presence, Scarlet quickly figured out how that could happen.

Scarlet took a deep breath and shifted to get more comfortable sitting on the floor in her skirt. Tyr stood quickly, picked her up, put her in the chair, and sat near her feet. Scarlet sat speechless at this strange action. The others watched but thankfully kept silent. When Scarlet could form coherent sentences again, she looked back to her companions.

"We need to double security on the seals. We need to keep them on our persons and safe until this threat passes."

"How are you going to carry around a long sword discreetly?" Bianca asked. "And you don't have to try to hide a crown. I mean come on. There are very few things one can wear a crown with, especially one that can end the world. Even in New York."

"We will conceal them. We didn't have to use our magic before as we never needed to hide the seals. Now we do. We can turn them into something else and hide them away like ordinary objects," Death said.

Scarlet nodded and the others followed suit. They never needed to employ concealment on their seals, but if the time ever came that required such a precaution, they had the ability. Scarlet wasn't entirely sure what she would turn her seal into in order to both conceal it and use it if she needed, but maybe Tyr could help her figure it out.

The thought surprised her even more than him picking her up off the floor. When did she stop thinking of *I* and started with the *we*? It was unnerving how he had been back in her life only a few hours and already commanded her mind and body. Scarlet wanted him. Even now, she longed to feel his fingers on her skin and run her hands through his hair.

Thankfully self-control and discipline had been instilled in her since her creation. She kept her urges in check for the time being. No doubt Tyr would gladly volunteer for anything she asked that involved touching him and vice versa. Even before he'd never been able to keep his hand and lips off her. During sparring especially, she'd had to box his ears more than once to halt his wandering fingers on her cleavage or creeping up her inner thigh. She swallowed the memories and tried to get back into the matter at hand.

"I'll turn my crown into a pin and just wear it on my shirt at all times," Bianca said.

Katherine sat forward and pursed her lips. "I suppose I can take my scales to work and turn them into a decoration. Just downsize the scale in order to be able to bring them back and forth. Or I could make them into a keychain." She looked pensive for a moment. "Yes, a keychain."

They all looked at Scarlet. "I suppose I could turn my sword into a pen. It would be easily concealable, and I could carry it with no problem."

They all nodded before looking to Death. She had her forehead wrinkled and stared at the floor shaking her head. "I honestly have nothing. I really can't hide my seal."

Bianca interrupted her. "Well, you could tell us what your seal is and then maybe we could help you work it out."

"Um..." Death looked between them.

Katherine spoke up this time. "She has a point. It has been a very long time. You have to trust us by now."

Cloris tensed, her shoulders tightening as they always did when she was under pressure. "I do trust you. All of you, with my life."

Bianca asked the question burning in all their minds. "Then why is it such a big deal that you can't tell us?"

Death bit her lip. Another sign she was in distress but didn't want to vocalize it. "It is not my decision to share it with you."

Scarlet looked around at the others. Everyone wore an equally confused look except Death who just looked sad.

"For Christ's sake," Hades broke in. "It is my decision whether she tells you all what her seal is, alright."

It was the first time Scarlet had heard his voice above a whisper, and she realized how this man could control an entire realm. His voice washed over them in a wave. Scarlet recovered enough to speak first. "You have been with us as long as she. You can't say you don't trust us."

"It's not that I don't trust you; it's because you're women," he said as if that answered everyone's questions.

"What does that have to do with anything?" Bianca asked.

"Woman are unreliable when it comes to beautiful men. I have never in my life met a woman who did not fall in love with me instantly...save Death."

"Is that why you hate her?" Bianca asked, voicing the question that plagued them all for two millennia. She always put a voice to the hard questions.

Hades took a deep breath and locked his jaw. The most outward sign of emotion Scarlet had seen on his face in decades. She also resented the fact that he said everyone fell in love with him. It pained her he thought he meant so little to them. It might be their own fault though, they didn't go out of the way to make him feel included. He wasn't a horsemen. He'd simply showed up the day they were created, and that was that.

Hades stood to leave, but Death reached out and clutched his arm. He ripped it from her grasp and stepped forward as if to strike her. Everyone surged to their feet, including Tyr.

"This is why I said she couldn't tell you. You all treat me as an outsider even though I have been with you since the very beginning. I would never strike her, ever."

"Hades," Cloris said in an attempt to placate him.

"No, don't speak me in that voice of yours. I'll not be bewitched. You all want to know why she can't transform her seal?"

They all stared waiting for the bomb to drop. "Because it's me. I'm Death's seal." He said it glaring at them all, one by one, and then stormed from the brownstone. The door slammed in its frame hard enough to rattle the windows.

The news shocked Scarlet to her core. She'd never even considered what Hades' presence was to them and what his place might be in the end of days. Of course they'd all read the prophecies, but Death's had always been sort of vague, as was the whole damn book. She shifted before sitting back down in the chair. Everyone else followed suit.

"Well, are your gatherings always like this?" Tyr asked.

"I wish they were," Bianca said. "We might actually accomplish something and say things that weigh heavy on our hearts." She turned a pointed stare toward Scarlet.

"Come on, are you really going to get on my case because I had a secret husband?"

"It sounds like the headline of the Maury show." Bianca giggled.

Scarlet shrugged. Nothing could be done about Bianca or her attitude, and she doubted even the end of days would be able to squelch it.

"What should we do about Hades?" Bianca continued.

"Nothing," Cloris cut on. "I will handle Hades. You all might not see it, but Hades and I work well together. I'll fix this, and he will be more polite next time."

Scarlet didn't know if that was a promise or a threat.

Chapter Six

The gathering resumed it's silence while they all considered Hades' confession. Eventually everyone looked to Death who sat with her hands tucked under her knees like she was used to this sort of behavior.

"What? He didn't want me to tell you guys. I figured I'd at least give him that courtesy."

Scarlet spoke up again. "How in the hell could you have kept a secret like that for two thousand years?"

Death shrugged as she crossed her legs and arms leaning back into the couch. Her posture clearly said, *you will get nothing from me*.

Katherine spoke up. "Well, then we will have to take turns to protect Hades. If he can't be transformed into something more protectable, we will just have to do it the old fashioned way."

They all nodded in agreement, and Scarlet stood. "I think we should go. I'm tired, and I'm supposed to be at work early."

They all groaned. Bianca threw a plush red pillow at her face, which she dodged neatly. Tyr stood up off the floor and nodded to them all in turn.

"So formal," Bianca quipped. "I like him."

Tyr smiled at the tiny immortal. He wanted to know her age, well, why she looked so much younger than the others. Bianca held secrets, ones she kept hidden beneath a shiny veneer of brutal honesty and sarcasm. He hoped one day she would consider him a friend enough to confide in him. That went for all of them. They were friends and eternal companions, but that didn't mean they all did not have their own secrets to protect. Hell, he himself had been one of Scarlet's for a long time. It was nice to finally be out in the open. He took full advantage of it, stepping up to take Scarlet's hand in his own. She looked down between them and up in confusion. But she didn't pull away, and that was enough for Tyr.

"Let's go," she said. Hands entwined, she all but dragged him from the house.

"I would take you on the subway, but I fear you wouldn't fit," Scarlet said staring up to the top of his head pointedly. "Also that you would seriously frighten the other passengers."

"I'm wearing a suit, how frightening can I possibly be at this moment?"

"You're a large bearded man missing an extremity. Your appearance, although tidy, doesn't necessarily inspire comfort."

"Is Justice meant to be comforting?"

"Can the philosophy wait until we get home? I need food and a shower and coffee...not necessarily in that order."

He nodded as they climbed into a taxi and headed back toward her place. Tyr stepped out of the taxi first on high alert for another hellhound, but the twilight cast innocuous shadows across the ground. Nothing waited for them in the darkness.

She led him to her apartment, and as he ducked slightly upon the threshold he realized she hadn't been exaggerating. Her apartment was small. Also one room made up the entirety of the place. His heart threatened to break seeing her live like this when the others lived more lavishly. Scarlet would probably decline assistance from them, but she wouldn't dare decline her own husband.

"Pack your bags." The hollow tone of his voice belied the anger surging through him as he spoke. His heart took up a heavy beat as his anger rose, but he held it back so he didn't shout at her on the first day of their reunion.

"What?" she asked and tossed her keys on the table.

"Pack your bags now. We are leaving this place."

"This is my home."

"No, no, it is not. You're telling me you left me, my home in Asgard, everything to live in a hovel without any support from your friends. This is preferable to asking for help or taking charity from others?"

"Yes," she said turning to square off with him.

His voice rose steadily as she tested his patience. "Pack your bags, or I'll do it for you and drag you out of here."

"We're not in Asgard. You can't force me to do anything."

He suspected her resistance was more in response to his forceful tone than the actual leaving. Tyr attempted to moderate his voice. "Scarlet, I would prefer to sleep in a place that is able accommodate my height from wall to wall. I would be more comfortable somewhere else, and I would be very happy if you would join me."

She eyed him belligerently with her arms crossed under her breasts in defiance. Her gaze said she was skeptical of his motives, but she turned toward her bed and pulled out a bag from underneath it.

He watched as she grabbed her necessities, which seemed to be almost all of her belongings. Scarlet turned to walk out, but he grabbed the bag and slipped it over the curve of his left arm. It weighed nothing to him. As they left, she stopped suddenly and went back to grab a great sword from behind her door.

"You keep one of the seven items used for Ragnarok behind your door?" he asked in disbelief.

Scarlet shrugged. "It discourages intruders." She held the sword in her palms and closed her eyes. In moments the sword transformed into an ornate navy blue ink pen resting in the palm of her hand. She slipped it into her purse and walked out the door.

In his many years he would never understand women, immortal or not. A heavenly object clunking around against lip-gloss and feminine hygiene products took some of the mystique out of the situation.

They traipsed back to the curb, and he hailed a cab. Tyr was beginning to think he missed his calling summoning the yellow vehicles. Once inside, the driver asked where they were going. Tyr turned to Scarlet and took her hand in his own.

"My dear, I need you to tell me where a hotel is. One that I would enjoy staying in, not one that you would prefer to stay in to spare me the expense."

She pursed her lips and remained silent.

"Fine," he turned back to the face the front to address the driver. "Take me to the grandest hotel in this fine city."

The cabbie pulled away, and Scarlet gasped. "You can't. Besides I doubt they will even have a room for you. These places don't rent by the hour."

"Well then perhaps when I ask you a reasonable question you might give me a answer rather than remain silent."

She huffed and turned to face the window. Back in their marriage for one day and they were already fighting.

They arrived at a hotel called The Palace, and Scarlet grabbed his arm as he tried to get out. "We can't stay here. I don't even think I can walk in there looking like this."

"We will stay here. If it makes you feel any better you can pay for the taxi."

She sighed loud and passed money up to the driver before getting out behind him.

They entered, and Tyr decided this was more like it. She should be living in a place like this. He walked to the front desk lined in ornate gold plating and beautiful marble. The elegant gentlemen standing behind looked him over before addressing him. "Can I help you, sir?"

"I would like a suite, please."

The man tapped on his computer. "And how long will you be staying with us?"

"Open ended stay, I'm afraid. Can you please find one I can book for some time?"

"Of course, sir, we have a number of extended stay suites. Will it just be you, or will you have a guest?"

Tyr dragged Scarlet toward the desk. Once upon a time she would have looked down at this man as if she were a queen. Now she stood cowering at the opulence of the place. Tyr's jaw hardened, and he resolved to fix her no matter what it took. "My wife will be staying with me."

The man gave her a quick look but said nothing.

Tyr slid his credit card across the counter, and the man processed it.

"It is a pleasure to have you with us, Mr. Asgard. Please let us know if there is anything you need." The man slid back his credit card and a set of key cards in a gold embossed envelope.

"Thank you." Tyr hiked Scarlet's bag onto his shoulder and grabbed her upper arm in case she felt the urge to flee. They went to the elevator and up to a room with an amazing view of the city's skyline.

When he closed the door, he tossed her bag to the floor and turned around in an attempt to control his growing anger. "What is wrong with you?" he shouted, unable to moderate his tone.

"What do you mean, 'what is wrong with me?'"

"You're acting like some damned wounded animal. You're Scarlet, wife of Tyr, Horseman of the Apocalypse, and the embodiment of War itself. You cower to no one. You bow to no one. And yet I thought you would melt into the floor as we stood before the check-in desk downstairs. You're not the woman I married. What the hell did you do with her?" For a moment Tyr feared he'd gone too far, but even so he felt justified in trying to piece together why she was acting like this.

"I don't know," she replied in a tone that made him want to shake her. "I don't know. I have been trying to figure it out for myself for some time.

One day I became this person, and I haven't been able to go back." She turned away from him, and he thought she might cry. But that would be impossible.

"I don't want to fight with you." Tyr approached her back and ran his hand down her arm. "I came here to be with you. I want to spar with you, make love to you, and be your partner in whatever battle you're currently facing. I still love you even after everything you've put me through. Just let me be with you, please." He hated the note of hysteria in his tone, but he needed her to see how much he needed her. She may think herself immune to everything, but he wasn't. Her touch could bring him to his knees. He would even give his only hand, his life, anything. All she had to do was ask.

"Why? Why after all this time do you still love me? After everything, your search, your sacrifices...how can you still love me? I don't think I can forgive myself. How can you?"

Tyr spun her around so he could look into her eyes as he spoke. He needed to be absolutely clear and ensure she heard him as he spoke the words. "I love you. I have loved you since you first challenged me. You're my wife and my life. There is not a single thing I would not do for you. Except leave. That is something I'll never do."

Scarlet held his gaze for a few nerve wracking heartbeats. "Please," she whimpered before stretching so he could meet her lips with his own. He didn't hesitate for a second but pulled her into his arms, completely enfolding her into his embrace.

She tasted like Asgard, like home, and when she parted her lips to allow him access, he felt the towers of the palace and the walls encircling his favorite garden. He didn't need Asgard when he held her. She whimpered into his mouth, and he broke away, his breathing heavy, and attempted to regain his composure. "My love, did I hurt you?"

Scarlet looked down at the floor and shook her head. When she raised her eyes to meet his gaze again, a fine sheen of tears coated them. Not a single drop fell, but it was enough for him to know that he affected her as well.

"I love you, Scarlet. I will always love you."

There was nothing else to say. She kissed him again, and he lost himself to those plush lips and her roaming hands.

Chapter Seven

It had been so long since Scarlet felt this surge in her blood, this need for another person. Hell, any need at all. Compounded with his absolute intent to take care of her, Scarlet worried for a moment she'd died and gone to heaven. If she even went to heaven, she wouldn't have known. Technically she didn't have a soul so...she shook the thoughts from her mind and focused on Tyr's lips.

He let her hands roam up his back and down his ass as he kissed her. She loved every hard curve of his body pressing against hers and slid her fingers into his hair pulling it through her hands. It was soft and warm as she cupped the back of his neck her hands still entwined in the strands.

He delved deeper into her mouth pulling her close. Part of her warred against her eagerness to touch him. The other half wondered if she was ready for this. When he backed her further into the room, she broke the kiss and stepped out of his embrace. He looked at her, the question clear on his face.

She ran her hands down his arms to soothe him. "I want to shower and eat. I need some time to get used to this again."

Tyr reached out and ran a thumb across her swollen bottom lip, and she cupped his hand. "I'll order something to eat while you shower."

She nodded and searched for the bathroom. It was exactly as you would imagine the palace bathrooms to look complete with beautiful white marble, gold leaf accents, and clear clean glass. She ran her hand across the vanity top and up onto a neat stack of fluffy, white towels. They were folded perfectly, one stacked on top of the other.

Scarlet turned on the faucet in the shower. After the water warmed she flipped it to the showerhead. The droplets hit the glass and slid down as steam poured behind the shower door. She stripped anticipating the hot blast of water on her stiff muscles. Stress always made her stiff and sore, and today had proved to be more stressful than most.

The main spray hit her back in a fine blasting fan as she stepped behind the glass. She sighed aloud as the water coaxed the knots from her shoulders allowing her to release some of the tension that had wound her tight since Tyr's arrival. It sure beat the plastic shower curtain from her old place. The steam built up slowly as it fully immersed her in the heat and damp she often sought solace in. Long, hot showers were her one luxury.

The door handle rattled, and Tyr entered. She was tempted to duck further into the steam, but after a few seconds the action seemed ridiculous. He'd seen every inch of her more than once and never once complained about her appearance. She locked eyes with him through the glass as he approached staring enrapt as water cascaded down her body.

"You lost weight," he said, leaning against the vanity countertop so he had full view of her. "I noticed earlier, but I did not think it appropriate to say anything at the time."

She didn't really have an answer to that so she remained silent, dropping her gaze to focus on washing her hair. As she lathered Scarlet felt his eyes on her. When she finally looked at him, the large bulge at the front of his trousers caught her attention. He made no move to hide it and showed no shame. That was something she missed about non-humans. Humans seemed to feel shame for everything they did, even if it was enjoyable. *Oh I ate a piece of cake and now I feel terrible about myself. Oh I read a good book; that was a waste of time.* Tyr's complete lack of shame turned her on. Or it might have been the kiss. Heat snaked through her, and a wicked feeling consumed her. She might not be ready for sex, but she could do other things.

After she finished rinsing her hair, she licked her lips and met his gaze which he eagerly accepted. But he dropped his gaze as her hand trailed down her body to rest in the curls at her core. She parted herself to rest her finger on her swollen clit. It had been a long time since she allowed herself this, but it wasn't really for her. It was for him. Scarlet wanted him to see that she was still a sexual creature, and that she still wanted him.

In turn he unzipped his pants and delved his palm inside. She couldn't see all of him through the fabric and his grip, but the glossy pink head stood tall above the waistband of his pants amplifying her own arousal. He matched her swipe for swipe as she circled her clit sending pulses of lighting through her veins. He pumped himself inside his pants as she watched.

It didn't take long with such beautiful visual stimulus before she felt the slow, hazy edge of her orgasm creeping on. She circled her clit faster adding a third finger and bracing herself against the shower wall for balance. As she clutched her hand between her legs and rubbed harder, Scarlet watched him move faster. He bit his lip, and she knew he was on the edge of his own orgasm. After a moment all thought fled, and she broke apart against her hand. She closed her eyes as the sensation washed over her in a chill juxtaposed against the wet heat of the shower spray. It was a soft, gentle wave that ebbed back slowly. As she removed her fingers, she opened her eyes to see he had spent all over his hand.

It felt good to see him undone. His hair was wild, cheeks pink, and his lip red where he had bitten it during his own climax. He washed his hand and redid his pants without a word, but she wasn't finished with him yet. She wanted him, and he was her husband.

The doorbell rang as she stepped out of the shower to approach him. Her shoulders slumped in disappointment, but the hard rumble of her belly reminded her she had time to fuck later. The food was here now.

He left to answer the door as she dried off and slipped into a robe. It was some sort of ridiculous terry material because it rested against her skin with the comfort of animal fur. As she exited, the delivery concierge eyed her, and she scowled at him. He would regret that look if Tyr saw it. Once the boy left with the tip, Scarlet curled up in a chair next to the table where the food was laid out.

"Dare I ask what that was that was about?" Tyr asked removing the silverware off his napkin and picking up the white linen to spread it on his lap.

Scarlet froze in the act of grabbing her own utensils. “What was what about?”

“The shower,” he said pointedly.

Realization dawned. He wasn't shy, but he probably didn't want to be graphic at the dinner table. "You miss me as I was before. I miss me as I was before. I want to be that woman again, and I think I can, if you help me. I don't think she's gone."

He nodded in agreement as he perused his food options and selected a heavy pasta dish. "I keep seeing her here and there. In small gestures or sometimes when you look at me. I would be very happy to return you to your rightful self. To be honest I think your friends miss you too."

"I don't know. They have changed since we've been here as well. I don't know what I'm doing. I'm supposed to be making a life here, but I feel like I'm in some sort of holding pattern, waiting for something. I don't enjoy my job; I barely eat. All I really do is work out, and I'm starting to hate that too because I do it so much."

"That explains the weight loss."

"And because I don't eat the same way as I used to. Food is expensive. Living is expensive here. I had to learn how to live on a meager salary."

"You would not have if you'd have accepted your friends' offers for help."

"When do I ever accept help?"

He nodded. Scarlet knew he'd been on the receiving end of her stubbornness before. He knew it well.

She stared down at the heaping plates before her. There was a five star chef in the kitchen, but she wasn't in the mood for the heavy steak he'd ordered for her. Instead, Scarlet grabbed the salad and ate it dry with her hands cradling the bowl.

He swallowed some of his food and stared at her with a severe frown. "Please tell me that is not all you're going to eat."

"I'm not in the mood for heavy foods right now. If I want more salad, I'll call for more."

That seemed to placate him because he dropped the subject and continued to eat. She watched him scarf down his entire plate of pasta. After he finished, he eyeballed some of her food, and she pushed her plate forward still clutching the salad to her chest.

"I would not take food from you."

"You won't be, eat it. I have this, and as I said, if I want more I'll ask."

Tyr nodded again and pulled her plate to his side of the table tearing into the steak. She watched him eat, this small act as comforting as if he held her in his arms. She'd spent countless hours watching the man eat and to be doing so now seemed both surreal and comforting all at once. After he finished a contented smile played on his lips.

"Are you finished?" He peeked into the empty bowl.

"Yes."

"Then let's go to bed."

"To sleep."

He chuckled. "Are you asking me or telling me?"

It felt good to smile, to feel something other than anger or despair. For a while Scarlet thought she'd bordered on the fine line of depression, but she wasn't quite sure if immortals could become depressed. She tried not to think about it.

She didn't answer him but pulled off her robe and climbed into the bed. Tyr didn't need encouragement. He stopped at the edge of the bed and eyed her naked body from her toes to her head. As he loosened his tie, he held her gaze. She squeezed her thighs together, slowing the ache, to keep from climbing him like a tree. His unfaltering gaze constituted a seduction and a challenge rolled into one. This had always been their game. More than love and lust, it was passion and power, a heady mix of mind games and sex. She wouldn't sleep with him tonight, but she would do a lot of other things.

His tie hit the floor, and his jacket followed. She swallowed to try to clear her mind as he unbuttoned his shirt starting at the top. The usual way they played, neither could show interest. They remained completely neutral to one another, and when one cracked (and it always happened), they lost the right to choose the evening's activities.

Scarlet focused on him and on keeping her mind and face blank. It was difficult to maintain her composure. She'd been without the touch of a man for three years, and he looked so damn good. He got the buttons undone and pulled the shirt from his pants with two hard jerks. She swallowed again trying to maintain her composure. The bastard knew exactly how much she loved watching him undress, and he took advantage of that fact.

As the shirt joined the rest of their clothing, she saw his erection pushing at the fly of his pants but flicked her eyes up to keep them focused on other things, simpler things, thing that were far less likely to make her moan out loud.

He almost smiled. The sexy dimple on the side of his face almost came through. The man knew his effect on her. The three years they'd been apart did nothing to him physically. He looked the exact same as the last time they'd seen each other. That night, so long ago, she knew she would leave him in the morning and made love to him all night.

She closed her eyes and recalled the heavy weight of his body above her own, the rough scratch of his stubble against her cheek, and the fan of his breath against her neck. Most of all she remembered how he whispered *I love you* into her ear at least a hundred times that night. Her heart shattered the moment she climbed from that bed. Part of it remained on that pillow as she walked away. The morning sunrise always reminded her of that day. Something intended to be beautiful only hurt.

"You know closing your eyes is cheating?"

She opened them and met his gaze.

Tyr must have seen the sorrow because he dropped all pretense of play and gathered her into his arms. "My love, what is it?"

Scarlet shook her head until he pressed around her, and she burrowed into his bare chest.

There was no way she could hold it back now. She cried, sobbed, and broke apart as he held her.

Not once in her life had she cried. Not once. Yet she sat in her husband's embrace, a witness' embrace, and tears streamed down her cheeks in hot waves. They came forward as if the dam inside her had broken allowing them to finally fall. She sobbed against his shoulder, and he held her singing a ballad that lulled her into sleep. His rich deep voice comforting her, telling her she was safe.

Chapter Eight

Tyr woke with Scarlet in his arms. It was his single happiest moment in years. She'd cried herself to sleep, and at first he didn't know what to do. She'd never once cried. Even when she'd been stabbed in the stomach by a crazy Valkyrie just after their wedding, she hadn't shed so much as a tear.

This new sensitive side of Scarlet scared him, but at the same it brought a sense of relief. She always guarded that part of herself, even when they'd met. She never once let him in, and he felt like finally she might.

He didn't move for fear of waking her even though his arm had lost feeling long ago. Sunlight bounced off nearby buildings and streamed in landing softly against her cheek. She was so beautiful it made his chest ache to look at her. The last time he'd held her like this, they lay exhausted across his bed, the night breeze blowing through the curtains. They'd made love with a furious intensity that night. Had he known she would be gone the next morning, he would have chained her to his bed until he'd talked some sense into her.

She stirred in his arms then sat bolt upright and looked around. When her eyes rested on him, his heart seized for a moment. He sat up beside her and shook out his arm. "Are you okay?"

"Sure." Scarlet nodded looking around the room and then over at the alarm clock beside the bed. She turned back and then jumped up, throwing the covers off her naked body and racing toward the bathroom. "I'm late for work."

Why she wanted to go work, he had no idea. She didn't like her job or her colleagues, and he was more than willing to provide for her.

In the meantime, he could help relax her. He stood and divested the rest of his clothing into a pile on the floor moving toward the bathroom. She stood naked in front of the mirror brushing her teeth furiously.

He leaned against the doorframe and let her wide gaze travel up his body. "Why are you going to work?"

She shook herself back to her task. When finished, she spit the foam from her mouth and turned on the shower. "I have to make money and survive here. I have to."

"You say it as though people doubt your ability. Why do you torture yourself in such a way when I'm more than willing to care for you?"

"What am I supposed to do? Sit around and let you feed and clothe me? I can't do that."

"Then do something else. I would be more than happy to unclothe you and feed you, but at least you could focus on other things like trying to find something you're passionate about. You could try something new at your own leisure that would make your life more full, make you happier. I know you don't want to work at Katherine's café, and that is fine. But you also do not want to work for that dreadful, squat little human either. I know it."

He watched Scarlet war with herself. She hung her head and clutched the side of the sink. Tyr allowed her the time. She'd done the same thing the night he'd asked her to marry him. That time she didn't say anything for twenty minutes after he'd asked. She liked to think things through, and he possessed the patience to let her. This time she didn't make him wait quite that long.

"You're saying you will take care of me. Ensure I want for nothing while I search of a pastime I enjoy?"

He nodded.

"Why?"

"Have you lost your brain, woman? I'm your husband, and I love you. I took an oath to care for you, and you have deprived me of that ability for far too long."

"Fine," she said with a short pause. "I'll allow it. For now."

He smiled and swept her into his arms. She wrapped her legs around his hips as he gripped her ass with his one hand and held her waist with the other arm. When her lips met his, he savored the taste of the mint toothpaste on his tongue because hers had delivered it there. She broke away breathless, and he set her down.

"Want to shower?" she asked stepping into the glass enclosure with a saucy look. Oh how he missed that gleam in her eye when she was up to mischief. To his disappointment she really did want to shower and quickly finished the task leaving him wet, hard, and alone.

She wrapped a towel around her upper body and dried her hair with another. "Do you want to try this sparring thing again?"

He watched her as he lathered up his chest. "Don't you need to make a call?"

Her eyes flew wide. "Right." He could hear her in the other room. "Mr. Ericks, this is Scarlet. Sorry I was not in on time this morning. I'm just calling to say, I quit."

"What did he say?" Tyr shouted as he rinsed the rest of the soap from his skin before stepping out of the water and turning it off. He exited the bathroom to hear her reply.

"He planned on firing me today anyway." She shrugged and dropped the wet towel over the chair before grabbing some lotion and slathering it on her arms. He watched enrapt before she stopped and glared at him. "What?"

"Nothing," he said, sitting down on the desk chair to watch her.

"Even harbingers of the apocalypse need to moisturize."

"Of course they do."

She narrowed her eyes at him again before continuing her ministrations. He didn't get up for at least a few minutes after she'd finished because of the ache in his balls. He feared he would be unable to walk.

Tyr picked up the hotel phone and called the concierge. "We are going to need a personal shopper. Yes, we have a list. Male and female. Thank you." She turned to stare at him. "What? You need clothes; I need clothes. As much as I would love to keep you cooped up here naked and in bed, I figured you might have something to say about that."

"Indeed." She stretched then climbed on the bed and situated herself to braid her hair. He joined her and kissed the top of her head which she brushed away. "Stop, you'll mess up my hair."

He chuckled and settled back. "We don't have to be dressed to spar."

"You want me to hit you while you're naked? What if I...hurt you?"

"Like that will happen."

"I have done nothing but train for the last three years," she said with a smirk.

"Well, then maybe you have caught up to me."

Scarlet glared at him, got up, and walked to the open space between the living room and the dining room. Watching her settle into a fight stance while naked was the biggest turn on of his life.

"You know I can't fight you while you have a huge erection. It is too distracting."

"Distractions are everywhere. A good fighter learns to ignore them."

She pursed her lips but remained silent. He set up a fighting stance despite the deep throb in his lower region. He remembered his own words, *distractions are everywhere.*

Scarlet threw the first punch as usual, and he blocked it with his forearm easily. "Don't play with me."

"You very much want me to play with you." He grinned before stepping to the side and sweeping his leg out to knock her down. She didn't fall for it and danced gracefully away but not before jabbing him in the kidney with an uppercut. He groaned but shook it off before facing her again.

Scarlet beamed at him, and he saw the woman he'd married. So confident she believed even naked she could win a fight against a god. She threw a right hook which he batted away. She moved to knee him, but he blocked it and took her to the ground. If distractions were a problem before, it proved even worse as he lay between her open thighs. Naked flesh met naked flesh, and he almost groaned aloud from the contact.

"Ah ah ah, distractions," she teased.

He made to flip her so he could gain the dominant position, but she anticipated it and shifted so he did little more than grind his erection into her belly.

"Holy hell, woman. There is only so much distraction I can take."

She smiled and swiftly boxed his ears with her cupped hands. He shook it off, but in that second she gained the upper hand to wiggle out from under him and into a crouch.

He dropped face down onto the floor and spoke into the carpet. "I concede, woman."

"Ha ha!" she shouted and jumped up to stand before crouching back down and looking at him from the side. "Are you alright?"

"My balls ache for wanting you, woman. You tease me mercilessly."

"There is no mercy here."

"I figured."

The doorbell sounded through the apartment, and she ran to put on a robe while he rolled over onto his back to free his rock hard erection from the confines of the rough carpet. She laughed and tied the robe before answering the door. He heard her speaking to the person on the other side before closing it again.

"Are you going to stay there all day?" she asked after a moment.

He looked up at her and smiled. "If you come down here with me."

"Not a chance."

"Are you afraid?"

"Yes, I'm afraid you will peel this robe from my body and make love to me on the floor until the hotel receives a noise complaint."

"I paid well enough that a noise complaint should not even be an issue. I think we own the floor."

She rolled her eyes.

"Why is that a bad thing, my love?"

"Because I'm not going to go back to Asgard or the void, and I don't think you can stay here. I think you will miss home, and I'll be left here to fend for myself. I don't think I'm capable of giving you up a second time."

Hearing the truth from her lips felt like an out of tune piano finally hitting the correct note. "Finally, you tell the truth. Why was that so difficult?"

Scarlet shrugged. "I don't know. It's hard for me to admit my feelings when I have to keep them bottled up inside. I don't know what to do with them. I feel them for a moment and then shove them away. I think that's what happened last night. They grew too great and exploded into a very embarrassing display. I could be the poster child for why adults should go to therapy."

Tyr chuckled and climbed up to crawl across the floor on his knees. He touched her thigh and then kissed it gently. "You don't need to feel embarrassed with me. You don't need to feel shame with me. You only need to feel wanted and loved and happy. That is all I ask of you. To want me, love me, and be happy to be with me."

"Those don't seem like terribly hard demands."

"And they should not be," he said as he twirled his finger in a circle around her kneecap. He knew in a moment she would be reduced to feminine giggles when the sensation began to tickle. Tyr craved to hear her laughter. When it did not follow, he looked up at her concern.

It was a long standing fact Scarlet was only ticklish in that one spot. He knew something bothered her further when she pulled away from his touch. The woman always confounded him. Every time he though he was gaining ground, she found a reason to push him away. *Was it all for nothing?*

Chapter Nine

Scarlet turned her face away to keep the tears from falling. Last night they'd sprung free as if they'd been waiting all her life. She'd broken down, and luckily he'd been there to hold the pieces together until she could get up again. She absolutely wasn't a weepy woman. "I don't know how we can be together."

"If you don't stop making these outrageous declarations, I'm going to punish you." Tyr climbed to his feet with a groan.

"You wouldn't dare."

"I would bend you over my knee and spank you until you stop saying you're going to leave me. I would rather enjoy it actually."

He said he would, but Scarlet knew him well enough. He would never dare touch her like that.

"My dear, right now you're thinking I would not dare hurt you like that, but I have news for you. That was the man you used to know. That man did not scour all the realms searching for you. The man you imagine me to be no longer exists. I'm a new man, and this one will bend you over his knee and spank you until your screams summon the human law enforcement."

She still doubted it, but a tiny part of her didn't want to push it. "Well, my decision stands."

"Why do you feel the need to tell me what I will or will not do? What I do or do not want? I'm a grown man, a god, and I can make my own decisions. If that means living here for the rest of eternity so I can be with my wife, so be it."

"You say that now," she said. "But you don't know how you will feel in a few months or six months or five years."

"And neither do you."

Scarlet grew weary of the conversation. They needed to get out of the room before she did allow him to make love to her on the dining room floor. The doorbell rang again, and she appreciated an easy escape from the argument. She opened the door careful as to not show Tyr in all his glory to the wait staff, accepted the clothing, and tipped the concierge.

"Clothes." She laid them across the back of the couch. Scarlet picked out a cream sweater, jeans, and short brown boots. The materials were expensive, leather and cashmere. More than she'd ever imagined wearing in her life on Earth. He put on a pair of black pants and a blue button down shirt. If it were possible he looked even better clothed than unclothed.

"Well, we are dressed as you wished. What do you want to do?"

She smiled and thought about what they could do. For the first time in a long she had the day before her like a blank, open book to write what she wished. "How about we start with breakfast?"

He shrugged. It was a daft suggestion, as he could always eat.

They left the hotel wrapped in luxurious wool and fur before hailing a taxi, something at which he was growing quite adept. Inside the cab, he wrapped his arm around her shoulder and pulled her close to press his cheek to the top her head. She swallowed the swell of emotions threatening to choke her.

Is it too much to hope for a happy ending? She wanted there to be one, but the world showed her over and over that it couldn't happen. She'd witnessed countless human lives cut short from one thing or another. Hell, even the gods were incapable of happy endings. Why should she have one?

They arrived at the White Horse Café and climbed out. When she entered, Katherine stopped short behind the counter and stared at her with her mouth hanging open. "Honey, is there something wrong with you face? It looks like the possibility of a smile."

"Stop." She waved her friend away and sat at the bar counter on the other side of the register. Tyr followed, sitting on the side closest to the door.

Katherine handed Tyr a menu. "I know what you want, Hon," she said to Scarlet with a wink.

She waited as Tyr looked over Katherine's small menu. She thought about what he would possibly want and decided in her mind, but he surprised her.

He slid the menu toward the opposite side of the counter. "May I have a bacon and egg sandwich and some coffee, please?"

"Coming right up," Katherine said.

"You're eating bacon and eggs on a sandwich? Where is your side of bacon and your bacon entrée?"

He tilted her chin up with his hand and leaned in to kiss her, but at the last second he leaned over and bit her neck gently making her squeal out loud and squirm away. The room went silent while Katherine and Bianca stared openly at the pair.

She didn't mind the staring. Scarlet even felt a little happy about it as she often spent time sitting alone at one of those tables glaring at happy couples touching and flirting with each other.

When Bianca placed the plates before them, she stared until Scarlet glared at her.

"What?" Bianca blinked innocently. "I want to see how he is going to eat a sandwich with only one hand."

Scarlet rolled her eyes and started eating. Tyr laughed, picked up the sandwich in his one big hand, and placed almost half of in his mouth at once. When he pulled the rest of the sandwich clutched in his hand away, he gave Bianca a huge smile around a mouth full of food.

"Oh, I like him," she said before slipping off to refill their mugs.

After he finished chewing, Tyr watched her eat her own eggs. "It seems I have already won over one of your compatriots."

"Nope, you won them all over when they learned you were crazy enough to actually marry me."

"Is it truly that hard to enter your heart?"

"Apparently not for surly gods of justice with a mythical hand."

He laughed out loud this time. "Gods I have missed you." Tyr kissed her head gently and took another swig of coffee.

Scarlet pushed at his chest to dislodge him even though she didn't want to, but she still wasn't sure about her PDA boundaries. Bianca returned to refill cups and take plates away.

"Where do you want to go now?" he asked.

"Nowhere."

"You want to stay here all day?"

"I want to stay here with you and watch the humans run to and fro. I miss the old days sometimes, and that was one of the ways I felt a connection to home even though I'm here now."

He leaned back to settle in while draping an arm across the back of her chair. They used to play this game in the void. They would sit on the chasm and stare into the glass of Earth to watch the people. Humans held great capability for love and wonderment, but they also had great capacity for the maudlin and disturbing. Everywhere on the planet there was something different, and that was always something Scarlet envied about humans. They could be anything, go anywhere, and forge their own destinies. They were not bound to end the world at a moment's notice and ordered to take countless lives.

Scarlet supposed she was jealous of them and their freedoms. While she was an immortal and destined to live forever, she didn't have the luxury of freedom. More than once since coming to Earth with her friends, she'd longed for death. If she knew a way to end her own life, she would have.

What would that have done to Tyr? How would he have reacted if he found out he became a widower? Would it have hurt more or less than her outright leaving him? If he died or left her, she didn't think she would have the strength to survive it again. The first time she'd survived by her friends alone. Even though she constantly pushed them away, they helped her live. She would always be indebted to them. Not only for that, but for moments like this with Tyr. Times spent in love and wonder and feeling those moments so deeply she could barely contain it all.

The only thing raining on her parade was the fact that she didn't know when it would end. If Hel broke the seals and the world stopped, she would have no choice. She would not be herself, she would be War, the embodiment of war, meant to slay and kill and take peace from the Earth.

Even further if Tyr decided he didn't want to be here with her any longer that could very well kill her. She read a book once, and in it the main character had said, *"It should kill you, that loss of love, like a head-on car crash...but it doesn't."*

At the time those words had hit her heart because she'd felt the pain of the protagonist, and she'd worked out for hours after reading that, pouring her pain and anguish into punching bags. She fractured her knuckles that day, but it had been worth it to purge the pain.

Tyr delved his hand into her the hair at the base of her neck, and she dropped her head back to rest in his palm. He massaged her scalp gently, and she almost melted. The man knew what drove her wild. She suspected he could do that with any woman, if they survived long enough to enjoy it after Scarlet finished with them.

"What are you thinking about?" he asked.

"I'm thinking, if any woman ever tried to take you from me, they would be looking at the wrong end of my sword."

He chuckled. "There is not a woman dead or alive that I could possibly adore as much as you."

"Good."

He massaged her head a little deeper, and she had to clamp down a whimper threatening to escape. "I have a better plan," she said.

"Oh yeah?"

"Let's go back to the hotel...now."

A light entered his eyes, and he smiled a sexy grin before standing up and pulling her bodily from the chair to set her on the ground in front of him. "Let's go."

Chapter Ten

They didn't even make it in the hotel room door before they seized each other. Tyr pulled her into his arms wrapping them around her waist to get as much of her against him as he could possibly manage. She held onto his neck, and he all but carried her into their room.

Tyr didn't know what brought on this change, but he wasn't going to complain. His wife was throwing herself into his arms as he'd imagined since the moment he found her. He'd waited for this moment for two days...no, three years.

As he feasted on her lips, he lost himself releasing all doubts she wasn't real and that at any moment she would force him to return to Asgard, alone. Not that he would make it easy on her. She'd lost her leverage completely since he'd discovered her end game.

When she moaned, thoughts fled from his brain. He tasted her, running his tongue along the seam of her lips. She opened immediately, and he delved inside the wet heat of her mouth. The mouth that delivered countless acts worthy of perdition to his body.

She fisted her hands in his hair, and he dropped down to the couch on one knee lowering her beneath him. He wouldn't be able to stand much longer with her hands meshed in his hair. He pulled back to catch his breath. She would have him coming before he'd even released himself from his trousers. The woman had done it before...twice.

"What's wrong?" Scarlet asked letting her arms fall to her sides. Her lips were swollen and slightly red from his whiskers.

Tyr swallowed in an attempt to compose himself before sitting between her spread legs and lifting one onto his lap. "I just need a minute to catch my breath. I have not done anything like this for three years, woman. I need to go slow, or it will be over in a few minutes."

Scarlet nodded leaning back into the arm of the couch. Not even an entire minute of silence had passed before she turned back. "Are you ready yet?"

He laughed and surged forward so his hips pressed into hers and took her mouth with his own. He eased back a fraction, but only out of fear he might hurt her. They had been rougher before. She enjoyed a little pain on occasion, he remembered that much.

She pulled back and started on the buttons of his shirt, undoing them one by one. After she got them undone, she ripped the shirt from his shoulders and helped pull it off. Tyr sat at a disadvantage, as she was still fully clothed. He removed her hands and put them on her own clothing. Scarlet quickly took her boots off throwing them across the room. Then she pulled the sweater over her head revealing a smooth nude colored bra and a tight, toned belly.

He wanted to spend some time just staring at her, but she quickly reached between them to undo the buttons on his pants. She didn't try to pull them down his hips. He braced his arm on the couch beside her head and used his hand to pull the pants down and off. Released from the confines of the fabric, he groaned. They'd started chafing as soon as he gained an erection.

"You're not wearing any underwear," she said in surprise.

"Why should I?"

"Because you're supposed to."

"Who says? Who makes up these strange human rules that everyone seems to follow blindly? If I do not want to be confined to undergarments, I shall not. Do you have a problem with my nudity? Because a few moments ago you were enjoying it."

Scarlet shook her head.

"Good, any more complaints about should or should not, and I'll put it away."

"You wouldn't. You want this as much as I do."

Always challenging. He loved that about her. "I can, and I will."

She mimed zipping her lips. He raised his eyebrows pointedly drawing her attention to the fact that she was still confined to her own pants.

"Oh, sorry." She quickly undid the opening and slid them down, kicking them off between his legs. He was naked, and she wore only her undergarments. Even those were too much.

"Take them off. This is why I don't wear them. They always get in the way."

Scarlet grinned reaching around to undo her bra and then shimmied out of her panties. The woman had groomed herself short. Nothing but a small patch curls rested between her thighs.

"What did you?" he asked aghast. "Why on Earth would someone groom in such a way?"

"It is called a Brazilian, and you saw it yesterday."

"You're not from Brazil."

"No, but this is the trend."

"By Odin's beard, I do not care about human trends. You are not a child, and you will not do that to yourself again."

"You're actually commanding me on how to take care of my body."

He knew to tread carefully. Some challenges she enjoyed and were meant to test and push him. Others weren't meant to be started, and he feared this was one.

"But..." He hung his head knowing she would win this fight no matter the outcome.

"If you prefer it natural, I'll leave it, but only because it's your preference."

"Thank you," he said in genuine relief.

She laughed out loud. "Are you aware that men here find it attractive?"

"Considering I'm the only man that shall be availing myself, it is only my opinion that should concern you. Now, can you continue? This topic is only making me angry."

She chuckled and reached up to pull his face down to hers. He released the ire building in his chest and kissed her back with equal enthusiasm. Scarlet tasted as he remembered sprinkled with lingering notes of coffee that he didn't mind in the least.

When they broke apart, he trailed his lips down the column of her neck, scented with soap and his own smell. He claimed her all over again. Each small kiss he planted, in his mind, were marks of his conquest.

"Will you get on with it?" she grumbled pulling him away from her neck by his hair.

"I'll get on with it once I relearn every curve of your body, every dip of your skin, every scar you bear. After I have educated myself, then I shall relearn your screams as they echo off the walls."

She released his hair. He took that for permission and dipped his head further to the upper curve of her breast. He bit the top of the right globe, and Scarlet inhaled, drawing breath deep enough to lift him up as her lungs expanded. He reveled in the shudder that rolled through her when he released his teeth.

Tyr scooted down her body further to plant one soft kiss in the center of her taut belly above her navel. Her hands speared his hair again and pulled the sensitive tendrils at the base of his neck.

With every inch he moved closer to her core, he could feel her anticipation, as she grew tight, drawn like a bow in his arms. She shivered in his hands and he knew she waited for the moment his lips would meet her clit, but he intended to draw it out until she shivered in his hand. Instead of stopping at her nether lips, he moved down to her inner thigh leaving a trail of bites and kisses in his wake.

There had been a point in the past where she wouldn't have been content to lay dormant during his ministrations. She had pushed him away before mounting him and using him to her own pleasure. That had been the first night they met and the very instant he knew he would win this woman's heart or die trying. That could be a very long time for an immortal.

The current situation was much the same. He lay between her open thighs again, and he once more felt the need to prove something. But to her or himself? She'd walked out on him once before. Was she really that invested in their union or did she merely pity him like so many of the others? *Beautiful mouth but those hands...useless.*

Tyr swallowed the pain, the lonely nights, and the self-loathing, then finally gave her what she wanted. He parted her pussy with this tongue and with one hard swipe wrung a cry from her lips. He could bring her to the brink of oblivion and slide her right back down to begin again. He imagined doing just that. A punishment dressed as a fantasy. Torturing her for the time wasted as he looked for her, the time spent angry in an empty bed, and time he spent doubting himself. If he were a different man, he might have inflicted such a punishment upon her...if he were a stronger man. Instead he brought his hand up to cup her ass, tilting her so he could bring her to the precipice of orgasm before fucking her over the edge.

"By all the fates in hell, just stop," she cursed.

"I have only just begun."

"You're torturing me, and I think it's on purpose although I don't know why."

Perhaps he was stronger than he'd thought. Tyr sat up and removed every bit of his own flesh touching hers. He wanted her like nothing else in the world, always had, always would, but gods he didn't realize how angry he was at her.

"I'm still angry because you left me."

"But I..."

"I know you explained. I know you did it for your friends. I'm aware it was for noble reasons, but noble causes did not keep me warm at night and make me want to scream and shred my pillow when I woke in an empty bed every morning."

Her brow furrowed, but she remained silent for a moment. "So you no longer want me?"

He turned and clutched one of her hands in his. "I will always want you. Even when we are apart, I yearn for you. That is the problem."

"Then I don't understand."

She pulled her legs under her and sat up. He recognized that look on her face. Sorrow and understanding with just enough pity to make him angry all over again.

He stood pushing her hand away before running his own through his hair. The hair entwined between her fingers only moments ago.

"I need to know you did not leave because I'm not a whole man."

She snorted. "Who says you're not a whole man? I'll cleave him with my sword."

"But really. Is the only reason you left me because of your friends?"

"Yes, nothing else in the world would have induced me to leave you. Nothing."

"I need to know you don't pity me for the parts of me I can't give you."

Scarlet crossed her arms under her chest and tilted her chin forward. He knew that look well, and it never proved to be a good thing for him. Regardless, he needed the answer.

"I married you."

"'Until death do us part,' but in case you have not noticed, we spent three years apart and both of us still happen to draw breath."

"I don't know how many different ways I have to tell you how I feel about you or why I left. What do you want me to say? Tell me." She climbed to her knees in front of him. Her naked body drew his mind from anger toward pleasure.

"I don't know. I need to know you love me. I need to know if I give up my life in Asgard it will not be to chase a dream that was never mine to begin with. I need to know that you will not leave me again."

"You know who I am. What I do. If those seals are broken, I won't be me anymore. I won't be myself. I will be War, not Scarlet. Not a trace of what you love about me will exist. I'll be merciless, cold, and there will be nothing to stop it."

Tyr swallowed. He knew what she was, but he'd never contemplated actually having to face that part of her. Those seals needed to be protected at all costs. Not because he cared about the humans and their world, but because he cared about Scarlet and couldn't lose her. It might be the one thing to finally break him.

"I vow to you," he said, running a thumb down the side of her upturned cheek. "As long as I draw breath, those seals will not be opened."

"Thank you, but I don't think you have that kind of power. Besides, doesn't this whole thing work with belief? The Greeks, the Norse, me...we are only here by human divination. If suddenly the world shifted to believing in only unicorns, then wouldn't that become the rise of the unicorn gods?"

"I know what you mean, but it's not all black and white," he said, shifting so he could meet her eyes as they talked. It had been so long since he found himself engaged in pillow talk and cuddling, even though the topic of conversation needed some work.

"We are all real. We all exist, but the level of our power and influence increases with human interaction. However, if suddenly, no one on Earth believed I was real, then I would not just disappear. I would have less power, yes, but it is all a balance to keep the gods in check ensuring they do not decimate humanity and use Earth as their own personal spa. I know some who would do that if they could get away with it."

Scarlet considered it for a moment biting her bottom lip as she stared off into space. He could have contentedly stayed as they were, until she started up another round of conversation. "What about Death?" she asked. "Cloris never seems to have problems, and people don't usually worship death."

"There is where your friend has the advantage. People don't worship death, but they fear it, think about it, fantasize over it, and dread it. Some even long for it, but every single human on Earth thinks about it so often Cloris will have a never ending supply of power. At least until humans stop dying."

As the silence stretched between them, Tyr simply gathered Scarlet into his arms. She trailed her fingers through the light smattering of chest hair he possessed, and the last thing he remembered was her soft snore against his shoulder.

CHAPTER ELEVEN

Scarlet woke to the shrill ringing of her cell phone. It vibrated and clattered across her nightstand. With bleary eyes she peered through the fog of sleep at the too bright screen. "Bianca, is someone dying?"

"No."

"Then why are you calling at five a.m.?"

"I had a dream...about Tyr."

Scarlet sat up with a start, her heart immediately clogging her throat. Tyr's heavy arm slid from her upper body to her hips. The man could sleep through the apocalypse. He didn't even move. "What was it?"

"I dreamt he had his hand in a wolf's mouth."

"That already happened. He gave up that hand to trap Fenrir."

"No, the other hand."

Scarlet didn't know what to make of that. "He's prophesied to fight Garmr, and they're meant to kill each other."

"I don't know if it was Garmr or not. I couldn't tell. He stood with his hand in the mouth of the wolf, looked up at me with tears in his eyes, and then I woke up."

"Thank for calling me. If you get anything else, please call again."

Bianca hung up, and Scarlet lay back down cupping the phone to her breasts. Losing him wasn't an option. They'd only just begun to know each other again. Scarlet glanced over to his sleeping face. He lay carefree and oblivious to the horrors in the world even though he faced more of them than others. Faint lines framed his closed eyes and a faded scar sat high on his cheekbone. Before she could reach out and run her hand along the mark her phone rang again. *Bianca again.* "What, what did you see?"

"Nothing, I forgot to tell you to come to dinner tonight. Cloris told me last night."

Scarlet's heart, currently lodged in her throat, resumed its normal beat, and she fought the urge to crush the phone in her hand. "Goodnight, Bianca," she said through gritted teeth.

Bianca's response cut through the phone. "Morning."

The phone went dead again, and she stared at the ceiling. The world seemed silent, no horns blaring or lights flashing across the ceiling. Nothing but utter silence. She contemplated how she'd reached this point.

The thought of doing things at her leisure again seduced her into relying on a man for support, and that never seemed right to her. At the same time Tyr seemed happy taking care of her, but what if he wasn't around anymore? What if something happened to him? She supposed it didn't matter.

Scarlet wouldn't want to live if he was gone, but what would happen if she died?

When they were created, there wasn't a manual. She just knew they had to protect the seals. She'd developed her own thoughts, goals, and intentions. When Tyr came into her life, she was happy to have finally found someone to take her mind off the waiting. Scarlet didn't necessarily care for the human race, nor did she want to lose herself to a nothingness that would consume the world. Her options—if they could be called that—were slim. She rolled over and pushed Tyr hard.

His eyes popped open and fixed on her. "You're not bleeding."

She smiled as he woke up the same way she did...grumpy. "No," she said before scooting under his arm more so she was face level to kiss him. Scarlet wrapped her arms under and around his neck holding on tight as she kissed him with everything she could muster.

When they both finally drew breath, he broke the silence only previously pervaded with their panting. "I like waking this way, please do it more often."

Tyr slept naked, and his erection pressed against her under the covers. She swallowed all the fear and the reasons she should say no before kissing him again. He growled in her mouth. She melted her body against his so every part of her molded to him.

He pulled away and spoke, his warm breath fanning her lips. "Are you sure? Because if you make me stop this time, I think it will be classified as cruel and unusual punishment."

She laughed against his mouth. "If you stop, I'll kick your ass."

"That's my girl." He rolled her over and settled between her open thighs as he propped himself on his elbows on either side of her upper body. His weight, so familiar, and yet so foreign, comforted her. She arched her hips up into him trying to get him to move faster. He smiled and gazed down at her as if savoring the moment.

"Will you stop staring at me and fuck me?"

Tyr laughed and slipped his hand between them, delving into her folds. "You are so wet already." He moaned against her mouth and pulled his fingers away. She felt the gentle prod of the head of his cock at her opening. As he entered her slowly, she held her breath until he was fully seated inside her. When she exhaled, the sensations washed over her. She swallowed a moan. The man knew how to touch her, even when all he did was breath against her neck or whisper a carefully chosen word in her ear. He destroyed her composure with no effort at all.

When she realized he wasn't moving all she wanted was to squirm beneath him. Make him give her what she wanted. It was a game they'd often played, and she didn't want to lose her first time back in the saddle, so to speak.

When he leaned down and bit her ear, she lost control bucking up against him with a moan. Her ears were a direct connection to her sex. All he had to do was breathe on them, and she would be lost. The bite, however, sent her hurtling toward orgasm.

"Stop," she said, trying to decide if she meant it or not.

He read her mind and did it again. He didn't even need to fuck her, he could sit inside her and caress her ears with his lips, teeth, and tongue. She would orgasm in minute.

"I don't want to finish so fast," she said. He nodded relinquishing his attention to her earlobes.

After what felt like a lifetime, he withdrew his hips and reentered her. A carefully controlled glide that sent every nerve ending sparking toward ecstasy. This was home. This was paradise. In this moment, in Tyr's arms, Scarlet was whole and everything she ever needed to be, both for him and for herself.

He moved in earnest, and she wrapped her hands around to cup his ass as he shifted his weight up onto his knees so he could watch as he entered her. The covers had slipped away, the pillows askew. They lay in the bed of lovers, and she couldn't have been happier, even at five a.m.

They perfected this position long ago since it was difficult for him to maneuver her hips with one hand. He slumped slightly and draped her legs over his shoulders. She used them for leverage.

Scarlet loved to watch him as he fucked her. He got an intense look in his eyes and his brow furrowed as if in deep concentration. She loved the way he bit his lip to keep from crying out. On the rare occasion he did cry out, it felt like she'd won a victory, winning a game against a master.

His arms caressed the outsides of her thighs, and she closed her eyes as he moved inside her. He drew her from spiraling into her own mind by scoring her thigh just below her hip with this nails.

"Focus," he warned.

She laughed squirming forward against him. They both inhaled sharply at the change in sensation, and he gripped her leg surging up with his hips. It drew her waist off the bed, but the sensations that rocketed through her could only be called paradise.

Magic lived in these small moments. The feeling of him touching her, his scent wafting from her skin before she stepped into the shower. Small innocuous moments that held a much greater meaning, humans and gods alike seemed to forget.

He drew her from her own mind by pinching her nipple lightly before resuming his grip in her thigh. Tyr wanted her undivided attention. He bit his lip as he surged into her harder, and she knew he would come soon. She wanted to be right there with him. Scarlet reached down and twirled a finger around her swollen clit enjoying the way his eyes rounded as he inhaled deeply. A few swipes of her finger had amped her up to his level.

"Are you close?" she asked twirling her fingers faster. He nodded, his eyes fixed on the movement of her fingers.

"Good, because I'm about to come."

He groaned and cursed in old Norse "*Skkkkitttaa*."

Tyr threw her head first over the edge to her own orgasm with strong thrusts as he came inside her. Scarlet stopped touching herself and held her hand over her clit as she rode the wave of ecstasy. Her legs shook, and she removed them from his shoulders as he collapsed across her chest, crushing the breath from her.

"You have to move." She groaned, his full weight proved too much to bear.

He rolled off her, pulling out of her body sideways. She twinged at the sensation but quickly forgot it as she cuddled up in the crook of his arm. A place meant to cradle a woman's head after lovemaking.

No, not a woman's head after lovemaking. It was the place for *her* head alone.

Chapter Twelve

Dinnertime arrived all too fast. Tyr would have been content to spend days getting to know Scarlet again in every way, but she'd insisted. So he put on a suit, and they headed to Cloris' house.

The woman lived in a high security building on the Upper East Side. Tyr felt the doorman's stare as he escorted Scarlet to the elevator and up to the penthouse. Cloris opened the door with a smile that didn't quite reach her eyes.

"Come in," she said, stepping aside so they could enter.

Tyr gave her a short bow, and they squeezed past into a foyer, if apartments had foyers. Somehow Cloris' did. Marble columns lined the room and opened up to the living area. She had to own the entire floor. It made sense Death would be rich.

"I don't think I've ever been here," Scarlet whispered as he removed her coat. She wore a black dress that molded to her muscular frame and dipped low in the back. He wanted to strip it from her body, but he doubted her friends would appreciate the action so he resisted the primal urge. As beautiful as Cloris' home was, it didn't compare to a few more hours spent in bed with his wife.

Tyr gave their coats to a middle aged man standing to the side. The lines around Scarlet's eyes tightened, and he knew she felt out of place. He rested his hand on her waist and led her into the living room where everyone else sat dressed in suits and similar black ensemble, except Bianca who wore a blood-red jumpsuit and black stiletto heels with a matching red sole. She looked every bit the femme fatale if there were such a thing as seventeen-year-old minxes.

He bowed to the ladies and tipped an imaginary hat to Hades who stood off in the corner. Tyr sat on the end of a snow-white couch with his arm tucked around Scarlet.

"How often do you do this?" he asked the group of ladies.

Bianca answered. "Never. This is the first time."

Cloris entered the room with the rhythmic tapping of high heels and smiled at the collective. She was dressed in what Tyr might have allocated as business attire, but the way it hugged her hips and breasts oozed sex appeal. This collection of ladies was attractive he realized, and each had their own way of being sexy. He hugged his wife close and kissed her head before turning back to their hostess.

Cloris stood before them looking regal as ever. "I'm so happy you all were able to make it tonight."

Scarlet spoke up. "I believe we weren't given a choice."

Cloris glared at Bianca. "You always have a choice, my love."

Scarlet pursed her lips, and Tyr tightened his arm around her. For a group of people she'd left her entire life behind to join, they didn't seem that close. A palpable tension hung in the air.

"What is it?" Tyr asked. "Something has you all on edge. I can feel it."

Cloris looked down at her clasped hands and then up at Hades. She rocked slightly and looked up the ceiling.

Scarlet straightened in his arms. This mustn't be normal behavior for Cloris. "She never fidgets," Scarlet whispered against his neck.

"It was decided—"Cloris cast a glare toward Hades this time"—that we need to be more transparent in our lives."

They all sat in uncomfortable silence while they waited for Cloris to elaborate.

She continued. "I wanted you all to know that yes, Hades is my seal, the one I am to protect until the end of days, but we are also business partners. We started a business three years ago. It has grown exponentially in revenue and is world renown. Hence, my apartment."

"And what business is that?" Kat asked.

"We run one of the most exclusive sex clubs in New York City," Hades said turning toward the group, his arms crossed over his chest.

Kat continued her line of questioning. "How did you come up with that idea, and is that even legal?"

Cloris slipped her heels off and plopped into the couch. "Yes, it is legal as all the members are screened, vetted, and consenting."

Scarlet shifted out of his arms to face the women. "You and Hades run a sex club? Really? Why did you think that would be some big secret?"

"You didn't know," Cloris pointed out.

Scarlet tensed. "No, we didn't know, but it isn't like we care. We didn't need all this fanfare. You could have told us sitting at the café, and you would have gotten the same reaction."

Bianca laughed. "You're just unhappy you had to leave the honeymoon bed. You're finally getting laid again."

Scarlet blushed, and Tyr chuckled. "We are married. Nothing wrong with that."

Bianca stood and approached him. She leaned down and put her face only inches from his. "No, nothing wrong at all, Justice." She tilted her head to the side and stared into his eyes. He was more than creeped out, but he remained still as she continued.

"You will hurt her before it is done. Before you can be happy, before she can be happy. You will hurt her more than any other." Bianca stumbled back and landed on Cloris' coffee table. They all stared at her with equally surprised expressions.

"What the hell was that?" Scarlet demanded.

Bianca shook her head and held up her hands. "I don't know. I never remember it."

"Of course not, seer," Tyr said as the anger boiled in his blood. "You can bring down the world with a few words and then be immune to the consequences."

Bianca was angry too. He could see her pulse beating hard in her slender neck. "I didn't ask for this curse. It came with my seal, and I only read for my friends and family. If you can't handle your own consequences, then that's not my fault."

Tyr opened his mouth to hurl more words at her. Scarlet gripped his arm tight, and he stopped speaking. Apparently this was a touchy subject with them all.

"How old are you?" he asked Bianca.

"I'm the same age as your dear wife."

"Then why do you look like a child?"

Her blood red lips curled up in a sneer. "I look the age I was made, or perhaps I sold my soul to Hades to retain perpetual youth."

Tyr didn't know if he should take her seriously or if she joked. "What else do I need to know about you all?" he asked, louder so the entire room could hear. "It would seem there are a great many secrets here that I might need to know."

"We don't share our secrets with a stranger lightly," Cloris said fixing him with her intent gaze. He could already tell Cloris didn't like her people to be questioned or upset. At some point she'd become the leader of their little merry band and took that title seriously.

"You're Scarlet's beloved and therefore family, but it will take some time to get to know us, and us, you," Cloris added.

He nodded and cast his gaze to Bianca who sat with her head bent down between her knees.

"It always takes her a little time afterward," Scarlet said.

Hades left the room and returned with a glass of wine for her. He handed it over making sure his skin didn't come into contact with hers. He must have been at the receiving end of one her little episodes as well, or maybe thought not to be.

Bianca put the glass to her lips and tipped it back taking the entire thing in one long gulp. When she finished, she noticed the shock on Tyr's face. "What? I have no gag reflex."

"So," Cloris interrupted. "Anyone hungry. I think Char has served dinner."

She stood from the couch and led them into the dining room that seemed even more formal than her living room. Hades sat at one end of the table, Cloris the other. Everyone else filled the middle. Kat and Bianca on one side, and Tyr and Scarlet opposite.

"What are we having?" Scarlet asked waiting for the butler to place a plate before her.

"Nothing fancy," Cloris said.

That was an understatement. The plate before Tyr was heaped high with beef and noodles smothering a mountain of mashed potatoes.

He looked at his hostess. "I expected something else. This looks delicious though."

Cloris smiled digging her fork into her own meal. "Thank you. I was in the mood for some comfort food."

Tyr didn't need to be told twice and dug in. The seasoning of the beef paired perfectly with the al dente noodles and the soft mashed potatoes. After a moment of shifting so he didn't get his hand in the food, he laughed, put down the fork, and shrugged out of his suit jacket and then loosened his tie. Even though they were dressed up, all the woman had removed their heels and made themselves more comfortable.

The mood of the party shifted dramatically. While everyone had been uptight and tension-filled when they'd arrived, the atmosphere had become more comfortable. Tyr noticed the friends Scarlet had, and he reached down to squeeze her hand under the table. She smiled and squeezed it back while listening to Bianca tell a joke. The sound of a knife against a champagne glass interrupted the mixed chatter. Hades stood at the end of the table, and Char handed out champagne flutes.

"I would like to take a moment to apologize for my behavior the last time we were together. It is very apparent to me that you all gave up your lives and destinies. I may well be dead now if you had not. I know I'm a secretive bastard, but that stems from a life hidden away." His gaze held Cloris', "I appreciate you." He looked around. "I appreciate you all."

They all held their glasses up before clinking with the nearest people. Tyr caught Scarlet's gaze and then took a sip of the bubbling liquid. It was dry, almost bitter, but Tyr didn't mind. His eyes remained on his wife, and she truly looked happy. He wanted to pull her into his lap and kiss her senseless. Instead he turned to Cloris to distract himself. "So when do we get to see this club of yours?"

In her surprise she sprayed champagne from her mouth onto the table. "You to see it?" she asked, before wiping her lips, face, and the table around her.

"Why not? I like sex. Scarlet likes sex. I can't speak for the others."

Bianca chimed in from the other side of the table. "I like sex."

"Are you even old enough?" Tyr ribbed.

She laughed. "I have been old enough for at least a thousand years.

He bowed his head in defeat. "Touché."

"They want to see it," Hades remarked, his gaze fixed on Cloris. She nodded.

"What's the big deal?" Kat asked.

"It's fine with me," Cloris said.

Hades laughed. They all stared at him openly. Tyr even reacted to it, and he had never been attracted to men. Hades' laugh caused things to tighten in his lower regions. The only one who seemed unaffected was Cloris.

"For dessert then," Hades said grabbing his suit jacket off the back of his chair and buttoning it.

Tyr followed suit as the ladies found their heels and Char handed out coats.

"We can take my car," Cloris said as Char left presumably to get said vehicle. When they hit the curb, a black limo sat idling.

"I feel like this is what prom would be like," Bianca said as she climbed in first. "Oh booze!" They heard her yell from the inside as they all climbed in after her.

The inside was comfortable with soft fabrics and leather. A mini bar sat on the far side, and they all helped themselves to more champagne. The ride was relatively fast, only about twenty minutes in traffic. As they all filed out, Tyr looked around. They stood in an alley barely wide enough for the limo with a red door off to the side. A light shone above the door highlighting a doorbell.

As the car pulled away, Cloris walked up to the doorbell and pressed it three times in rapid succession. A small, brown-skinned woman dressed in a black corset, black tutu, and top hat opened the door. She nodded at Cloris and eyed everyone that followed, completely ignoring Hades as he followed up the group.

As they entered the club, the darkness assaulted them with complete silence. The only sound was the echo of their own footfalls and rustle of clothing as they walked down a long, dark hallway. Scarlet reached back to hold his hand. They followed behind Cloris until she stopped, pulled a key from her dress, and opened the door.

A row of locked boxes lined the wall beside them. "Please place all cell phones and any valuables you might want to keep safe in here," Hades directed.

"Are you joking?" Bianca asked.

He gave her a look in reply.

"Fine, fine." She fished things out of her cleavage and placed them in the box before twisting the lock and removing the key. The key hung from a long, gold chain which she placed over her head. It hung perfectly between her breasts. Tyr looked away. That girl was trouble wrapped in temptation. His wife on the other hand was temptation with short bursts of trouble.

They all followed suit each of them placing valuables and cell phones in the boxes and removing the keys to hang around their necks. Tyr tucked the chain holding his and Scarlet's things down his shirt, the cold of the metal brushing his skin making him jump.

The group entered an antechamber, also silent until Hades closed the outer door. Once it was locked behind them, they proceeded through the second door into bedlam.

From silence and darkness to an all-out party. Inside the room people clustered in groups around low tables, plush chairs, and settees in opulent velvets. Servers, both male and female, served beverages to the groups, as a burlesque performer disrobed artfully on the stage. The place had the feel of upper class bourgeois without clothing. Cloris led them to an empty table toward the back. So far Tyr was confused. He didn't see a single person actually having sex, and some of the patrons wore less clothes than the actual employees.

"This looks like a regular club," he said pulling Cloris in by her slender elbow so she could hear him over the slow jazz number playing over the speakers.

"It does because this is the open room. All the smaller rooms are available for other activities. There is no outright sex in this room, but the other rooms can be borrowed if clients decide they want to play."

Hades slipped in on the other side of Scarlet and took up where Cloris stopped. "There are five main rooms, each with antechambers: Tartarus, The Fields of Punishment, The Fields of Asphodel, Elysium, and Isle of the Blessed."

Scarlet laughed, and Tyr smiled at the sound. "You created your own Underworld."

Hades nodded. The servers descended upon them, and they drank more champagne while they chatted and watched the stage. Tyr was intrigued by the setup of the club and the clientele. Everyone seemed jovial and carefree here. But Tyr was more than curious about what lay outside this room. He leaned down to whisper in Scarlet's ear. "Do you want to investigate one of these rooms?"

She giggled. He didn't think in the years he'd known her he had ever heard her giggle. Laugh, definitely. Giggle, never. He looked down at her face and saw the pink stain in her cheeks. The woman was well on her way to being drunk. He laughed but worried for just a moment. Should the embodiment of War drink to such excess? Could she do anything while in her cups?

Tyr glanced at Cloris who looked them both over and gave a small nod. He supposed Scarlet was fine if Cloris wasn't concerned. Scarlet leaned in, ran a hand up over his knee and then along his inner thigh. He kept his face perfectly neutral as she stretched to bite his sensitive ear lobe.

None of the others seemed to notice the change in their friend. Kat lounged back across the couch surveying the crowd. Hades and Cloris spoke in hushed tones with their heads bent together as the music swelled around them. Bianca danced on the main floor grinding against a well-dressed man who looked twice her age.

He pulled Scarlet into his lap and kissed her deeply. Cloris said no outright sex, and there was no way he could maneuver her dress to do such a thing. He settled on the heated moans that escaped her as he plunged his tongue between her lips. She tasted like rich food and dry champagne. When she pulled the hair at the nape of his neck, he almost came in his pants like an inexperienced youth.

She kissed with a fervor, grinding into him and touching him all the ways she knew drove him wild. When he finally pulled away from her lips, he breathed heavily against the bow of her mouth trying to catch his breath. That was when he realized the music had stopped.

Glancing around, Tyr noticed that every eye in the place was fixed on them. Bianca broke the spell by starting a round of applause. If he still blushed, that would have been an excellent moment for it. His wife did however, and she flushed a becoming shade of pink and hid her face against his neck.

The men stared openly at his wife, the women at them both, and her friends smiled fondly at them. No doubt they'd never witnessed this version of Scarlet. He certainly hadn't. Maybe he didn't need to bring back the woman he once knew. He just needed to get rid of the one he'd found when he first arrived.

Scarlet shifted in his lap as the music started again rubbing against his erection. The look on her face said it was accidental.

"Do you want to stop?" he asked her.

"No," she said leaning in to kiss him again. "I never want to stop with you. That's part of the problem."

Tyr chuckled and cupped her ass to draw her further against his erection. He wanted to slide into her naked, wet folds, but he doubted Scarlet would want to try such a thing in their friend's club. He settled for some more kissing and enjoyed the way her taste changed from hers to theirs as their mouths met. She reached between them and cupped his erection through his fitted pants. He almost lost it then as her hands grasped him through the fabric. There was just enough friction that they could stay that way and she could finish him off, but he didn't want that. Not here. He wanted her naked and in their bed so he could hear her moans loud and insistent as opposed to having them fight against the music.

He scooted her to the side so he could maneuver her off his lap with his right arm. With a lingering kiss and reluctant eyes, she let him. "Don't worry. I'm not done with you yet."

Chapter Thirteen

Scarlet woke with a heavy pounding in her temples. Opening her eyes, she took in her surroundings in small increments. The light streaming in from the open curtains. Her hands tucked under her pillow, and her naked skin against the high thread count sheets. She was certain her hair was matted and the mascara had smeared under her eyes. Those concerns disappeared when she caught sight of Tyr. He sat at the dining table sipping a cup of coffee and staring down at a tablet. The man had the attention span of a monk. As he read he barely moved. Even when she sat up and the covers fell away, she needed to clear her throat to get his attention. He swallowed and a simmering heat entered his gaze as he raked it down her body.

She briefly considered climbing into his lap but rethought it as she remembered her current appearance. "I'm going to take a shower. Can you order me some breakfast?"

"Of course. I'm glad to see you're taking to this new lifestyle."

"I guess I just felt like I had to do it on my own, but you're here. And you're not going anywhere, so I don't need to do it alone anymore." She entered the bathroom with his smile following her.

Even though life on Earth would be nothing like Asgard, Scarlet hoped they could make a happy existence there amongst the humans and their friends. After last night she felt so much closer to the whole group and one step closer to forgiving herself for the mess she'd caused running away from Tyr.

When she stepped out of the shower, her headache had abated and her skin glowed a healthy pink. Water and food would set her right again. She couldn't recall the last time she'd drunk that much and never planned to again. How had Tyr gotten up and looked so dashing already? If she could hate him, she would just for that.

She exited the bathroom in a cloud of steam and went to get dressed. Hopefully Tyr hadn't made any plans because caffeine, water, and food were about to become her focus for the next hour at least. Tyr stood and pulled out a chair for her. She plopped into it tucking her feet up.

"Your food will be here in a moment," he said taking his seat again. He poured her a cup of coffee and even remembered how she liked it: black with two sugars. She loved him even more as he pushed the mug toward her, and not only because the man possessed the coffee.

"What do you want to do today?" he asked after she had taken a few hot sips.

"I have no idea. I guess we can wander around and see what happens. I like the idea of leisurely exploring the city. I know the city might not be new to you, but it definitely is to me. I've been working so much I haven't gotten the chance to check it out."

"In that case, I know the perfect place to take you."

"Oh?"

When he said nothing else, she prompted further. "Are you going to tell me?"

"Of course not."

She laughed, but the sound of the doorbell interrupted her. A server brought in her food and sat it on the table. When he left, she lifted the lid and found some scrambled eggs and white toast. Tyr was a saint. He'd even recalled her light eating habits. She enjoyed a good meal, but most of the time she didn't like to eat a lot in one sitting. It seemed to slow her down. "This is perfect, thank you."

He kissed her on the cheek and took his place again before continuing to read. He must have gotten the tablet from the concierge. It was a comfort seeing him assimilate to their new life. Not that she still doubted his intentions. It reinforced everything he'd given up to be there with her in that moment.

Scarlet ate in silence watching him across the table. Occasionally he would glance up and smile at her, but for the most part he read until she finished and pushed the plate away. "So, where to?"

He laughed. "Get your coat, love, and I'll show you."

As they left the hotel the early morning chill swirled through the tall buildings. A taxi pulled up in front of them, and Tyr made her close her eyes until they arrived. Once they stepped out of the car, she stopped and stared at the building before her. It looked vacant and for sale.

"Did you get the address wrong?" she asked.

He grabbed her hand and led her to the side of the building. "Nope, come on."

When she entered the main area, Scarlet resolved it was one of the most beautiful places she'd ever seen. Mats were laid out in every room. A completely empty sparring gym.

He grabbed a duffle off the floor and handed it to her. "Go change. We are finally going to have that match."

She stood up on her toes and kissed him fast before opening the bag and changing. He'd brought all her usual gear, and she wanted to squeeze him in a big hug. But even more she wanted to punch something.

Once she finished dressing, Scarlet found he'd changed too. He wore nothing above the waist, and his hair was pulled back in a rubber band. She could have skipped sparring all together seeing him like that.

"Ready?" he asked.

She just laughed and stepped onto the mats with him.

"I will not be easy on you." He moved in close to discomfit her.

"Ha. I won't be easy on *you*. You're going to need some Icy Hot later, old man."

"Woman, you can't be more than a few hundred years younger than me."

"Well, obviously those few hundred years make a difference.

He reached out to grab her, and she danced away. "I'll get you for that," he called after her as she rounded again to stand in front of him.

This time she went for him and took his legs out with a well-placed foot sweep. He hadn't even seen it coming. He went to his knees, but she was too focused on her victory. He grabbed her legs and ungracefully took her down. "It does not have to be pretty. It just has be effective."

She rolled out of reach and onto her knees. When he went to grab her, Scarlet threw herself to the side but not fast enough. Tyr threw himself across her torso pinning her to the mat. The man had never gotten this far with her. "Where did you get so good? You were nothing like this back in Asgard."

"That was years ago. I dove into training when you left to numb the pain."

She heard the heavy emotion in his voice. Dropping the fight, she reached up to cup his face and bring him in for kiss. He needed no prompting, moving so he could capture her lips better with his own.

Scarlet kissed him with everything she had, pushing all the pent up emotions and pain into the press of his lips. He took every bit of it, and when she broke away, his eyes seemed a little lighter, less filled with doubt. She hated the fact that doubt stemmed from her and resolved to spend the rest of her life trying to take that pain from his eyes.

She'd walked around this city pitying herself, and she'd never even consider the feelings he might have been feeling, wherever he was. Scarlet had no idea he'd searched for her, but she should have known. He wouldn't let her leave and forget about her.

Tyr pulled her up, and they sat side by side. She held his hand, entwining their fingers.

"This is for you," he said after a few moments.

"What's for me?"

"This place. I bought it for you. If I know anything, I know you're passionate about fighting. I thought you could turn this place into an exclusive gym."

She swallowed and thought about what he was saying. The man had bought her a gym. A place of her own. "When did you do this?"

"I got help from Cloris last night while you were, erm...passed out. She did not do much but showed me how to look for the place and what you might be looking for. When I found this, I thought it was perfect, called the agent, and made the offer. The man took it right away."

"This place must have cost a fortune."

"You could just say thank you."

She lunged at him throwing him back against the mat. Between kisses she said, "Thank you, thank you, thank you."

He laughed and kissed her back. "I'm glad you like it. I could tell, even though it's only been a few days, you were growing listless. You never did like to be idle."

"I don't like to be idle, but today I would like to spend the whole day with my husband. While you brought me here because you knew I would love it, I know somewhere I'd like to take you because I know you will love it."

"Oh?"

"Get dressed."

Scarlet dove toward her clothes. They dressed quickly before wrapping in coats and stepping back out into the chilly morning. For a moment she contemplated showing him the subway but thought better of it as he towered over her. He probably would look like a beaver stuck in a sardine can. Not to mention people would stare at his hand, and he didn't like that.

As they climbed in the cab, he asked, "Are you going to tell me where we are going?"

"Nope." She snuggled closer under his arm as the taxi whizzed around cars through the busy city streets.

He didn't appreciate the place right away, but as they stepped up to The Strand, she pulled him inside before the realization dawned. His face went slack in awe as he spun in a circle taking in all the books. The Strand touted eighteen miles of books, and she was certain Tyr would want to look at every single one. Justice was his calling, and while fighting was a part of that, he was an avid student of politics and Earth's history. He loved learning how people could create such disasters with a tiny spark.

She pushed him in further through the crowd. "Go, explore. I'll follow you."

He stopped and looked back. "But you will be bored."

"No, I won't. I like studying you, and besides you can make it up to me later." Scarlet gave him a wink, and he smiled before turning back to wade through the crowd.

As she suspected, he made his way to the bottom floor first. He ran his fingers across the book spines. She smiled at his joy. He was beautiful fighting, breathing, and even more beautiful caught in a wayward moment of pure abandon.

Scarlet walked behind him thinking about how glad she was he'd traversed the realms to hunt her down. He'd become her whole world, all over again, in a matter of days.

After several hours in the bookstore, it was well past lunchtime. Scarlet was starving. "How about pizza?" she asked linking her arm in his as they exited.

He'd been able to control himself enough to only purchase one book, but she didn't doubt he memorized every title he wanted and would return for them.

"That sounds good. I have never had pizza."

She laughed. "Then you're in for a treat."

They walked a few blocks until they found a mom-and-pop pizza place with a vaguely Italian name on the outside. She ordered, and he sat down. No sooner had the food arrived, when someone else joined them.

The hellhound sat down at their table with little fanfare. He was wrapped in a dapper coat, wearing a hat and gloves. On a regular street, she would've assumed he was just another pedestrian if it weren't for the scent of sulfur that wafted up from his clothes.

"What do you want, hellhound?" Tyr growled under his breath.

Scarlet stared at them both for a moment. She'd never heard him use a tone like that before.

"Answer him," she said reaching into her pocket to pull out a pen. She casually clutched it in her palm, but the hellhound noticed.

"Are you going to attack me with an ink pen, War? And here I thought we were just getting to know each other."

She didn't respond because she knew he was trying to bait her.

"I came at my mistress' bidding because apparently you little horsies have been developing a plan against her."

Scarlet's throat seized. How had they known that?

"I came to offer you one final chance to relinquish Hades. Do so and you will all be spared."

Scarlet did speak this time. "I'm not in charge of another being."

"Well, figure it out before I take a bite out of your little boy toy here."

Tyr's lip curled as he surveyed the hound. "You may be my undoing, but remember I'll also be yours."

The hound smiled a wide toothy grin before standing, buttoning his coat, and exiting the pizza shop.

Scarlet broke the heavy silence first. "What the hell was that?"

"That was Hel trying to get her way by brute force. She knows us and our lives. She's planning to use that knowledge against us."

"But how did the hound know we were taking precautions against her?"

He shrugged and stuffed half a piece of pizza in his mouth. She laughed, but the creepy crawly feeling still climbing up her spine kept her from enjoying it. Apparently, she was now acquainted with the other side of her husband's prophecy.

The pen was still clutched in her hand, and she shoved it back in her pocket. Scarlet didn't know if she could have drawn it with all the humans lurking at the edges of the store. She pushed the thought away. The day had been going wonderfully. She was happy, and nothing would change that.

Tyr sat happily eating his food and scrolling through the tablet he'd stashed in his coat pocket.

"What are you reading?" she asked nibbling at her own pizza.

"I saw a book about a fellow named George Washington, apparently a founder of this country. I wanted to read more about him. There is an unbelievable amount of information to be found on the Internet. Especially about this man."

She laughed. Scarlet knew who Washington was, but she didn't know much about the man. It was a comfort just to watch Tyr. He didn't seem terribly concerned about the encounter with Garmr though.

"Was that your first time meeting him?" she asked when he'd finished reading.

"Garmr? No, we met once before, but I remember his face."

"As one would when you're prophesied to kill one another."

"We both decided to stay far away from each other, and that was that. I don't know why he showed up here. Must be at Hel's orders since he made it clear he did not wish to encounter me again."

If Garmr didn't want to be there, but he was somehow under Hel's control perhaps they could make a deal with the hellhound themselves, free him from Hel's captivity, and ensure both he and Tyr stay alive. If he had any sense of self-preservation, he might at least consider it. She wondered how the heck she might get a message to the beast without Tyr or Hel knowing.

Perhaps Hades could help her. "I'll be right back. I'm going to call Cloris."

He gave her a vague nod as he resumed reading.

Scarlet stood and exited the shop. She called and waited impatiently while the phone rang on the other end.

"Hello," came a soft reply.

"Hades, it's Scarlet."

"Oh." His reply seemed more normal and not so wary.

"Do you usually not get phone calls?"

"No, never."

"Well, welcome to the 21st century. I need your help."

"Ok..." He drew it out as if he wasn't sure.

"Is there a way to get ahold of one of the hellhounds without Hel knowing?"

"I don't know..."

"If you're worried about Cloris, I can talk to her, but I would prefer to keep this between us. It has nothing to do with the seals, only Tyr and Garmr."

"You want to contact that beast?"

"I want to ensure the safety of my husband, and that's all. I think he would be amenable to making a deal or a trade or whatever to ensure he stays away from us."

"You met him?"

"Yes, he was here a few minutes ago threatening us for you, once again." The other line went silent. She couldn't even hear him breathing. "Hades?"

"I'm here. I hate that this is causing all of you so much trouble. It pains me that you're all in harm's way because of one crazy ex."

"I wouldn't call her an ex if she captured and forced you." The line went silent again. "I'm sorry, Hades. I didn't mean to bring it up. Can you help me or not?" Scarlet knew she sounded impatient with him, but she really needed the information only he could provide. If he couldn't help, she would ask Cloris.

"You might be able to send a Raven. But you will have to make it convincing when you send the message because the hounds will probably try to eat the Raven. So make it want to hunt the Raven and then allow the Raven to deliver the message."

"You think I'll be able to convince a Raven to do this."

"You might be able to convince Huginn or Muninn. They would be able to get the message there and get out safely. But be warned, the All Father will know what you seek to do."

"Why should that matter? You would think Odin would want to save his son."

"Well, that may well be, but the All Father is a purveyor of prophecy. If Tyr and Garmr are going to fight, he will assume the Ragnarok is upon us."

"Oh good lord, how much more convoluted can this get?"

"Good luck," Hades said before the sound of the disconnect cut through the phone.

She put it in her pocket. *Now to figure out how to convince one of the All Father's Ravens to take a message to a hellhound for me. No big deal.* Her phone rang in her pocket. *Cloris*. "Hello."

"Hades tells me you want to send one of the All Father's Ravens for a hellhound to hunt in order to send a message."

"Okay, when you put it that way, yes, it sounds bad. Hades is a rat too apparently."

Cloris laughed. "No, but there is nothing he can keep from me. Ever."

Scarlet shook her head at Cloris, even though she couldn't see the motion. "I just want to keep Tyr safe."

"We all do, honey. He's part of our family now. You don't have to hide the fact that you love him."

"I'm not hiding it, and not everyone would agree with this plan, especially Tyr."

Tyr tapped her on the shoulder. "What will not I agree with?"

Speak of the devil. "Gotta go, Cloris," she said before hanging up. She hugged him in an attempt to distract him, but it didn't work.

"What will not I agree with, Scarlet?"

"I was trying to plan a little get together, but Cloris doesn't think you'll like it."

He furrowed his brow and drew the hair out of her face with a finger. "I'm the god of justice. I can taste a lie on my tongue. I usually don't call you out on it, but this time I think you mean to hide something important from me. What is it?"

"Nothing okay, nothing."

"Scarlet..." His voice held a tone of warning, but she didn't know how to explain it to him in a way that didn't sound like a terrible plan.

"Can we go and talk about it back at home?"

He pursed his lips but said nothing as he stepped up to the curb to call a taxi. "I'll not forget," he finally said once they settled in the back of the cab.

Guilt and fear were heady emotions. They spurred humans into committing atrocious acts, and an immortal sat confronted with those same feelings. They seemed to be universal. She would do anything, *anything*, to save her husband. It was a scary truth to admit as her version of anything was for more dangerous than a human's.

Chapter Fourteen

When they entered the hotel room, Tyr removed his coat and sat on the couch, determined to remain calm. It had been less than a week since they'd been reunited and already she schemed behind his back. She sat opposite him in a large chair equally determined to not meet his eyes. At least she felt guilty about it this time.

"What were you were speaking with Cloris about?"

"Well..."

"Don't lie to me, Scarlet. Tell me what you're planning so we can fix it before you do something stupid."

She sucked in a gasp, and he knew he'd been too harsh with his words.

"If you're planning to leave me again, please know that I'll hunt you until the end of my days. And this time I will not be so forgiving."

"Oh gods, Tyr. I'm not leaving. I was speaking to Cloris to see if she knew a way to contact the Ravens."

"You want to contact my father's Ravens?"

"Yes. I figured if Garmr is equally unhappy to be killed by you, we might be able to discuss this is a civilized fashion before it turns to fighting."

He snorted. "War trying diplomacy. And what were you going to say to the hound? 'Please don't kill my husband. I kind of like him a little bit.'"

"Of course not, I was going to ask him to run away and hide until we figured out how to get rid of the Hel problem. Then you two could go on mutually ignoring each other. If that didn't work, then I was going to ask him not to kill you."

He sighed loudly, stood, and walked over to a bag she hadn't even noticed he'd acquired. Tyr pulled out a short glossy black feather that shone almost iridescent in the sunlight streaming through the open curtains. He dug into his bag again and found a box of matches. He took the items over to the sink off the side of the kitchenette and lit the feather. It flashed a blinding white, and they both cast their eyes away.

"What the hell are you doing?" she asked.

He shook his head and held a finger to his lips for silence. She shot him a murderous glare and pressed her lips together. Not even a minute passed before another flash of white light burst into the room. In its wake stood a beautiful naked woman with long, glossy black hair.

"Desire," Tyr said bowing at the waist.

The Raven didn't speak. She stood silent with wide eyes as she stared at Tyr and then at Scarlet who remained quiet as Tyr had bid.

"We ask a favor of you, Raven."

She turned her head to the side and stared at him. The Raven's voice sounded in his head. *"What will you ask of me, Son of the Great All Father?"*

"I ask you to carry a message to Garmr."

"You wish me to tangle with a hellhound?"

"I would not ask if it were not important."

"Do you believe Ragnarok is upon us?" After she spoke, she cast her glance to Scarlet. *"You have a rider here. Only one reason for a rider to be anywhere."*

"She is my wife."

"Son of the Great All Father. You married yourself to War. Justice and War, there is a poem there somewhere. What is the message you wish me to carry?" Tyr opened his mouth to tell her, but she held up one slender hand. *"I want to hear it from the rider."*

Tyr bowed again and looked at Scarlet. "She wants you to tell her what the message is."

"May I write it?" Scarlet asked.

The Raven tilted her head and nodded.

"Yes. You may write it," Tyr relayed.

Scarlet stood, straightened her pants, and went to the desk. Quickly she scribbled a few words and then handed the paper to the Raven.

"I may ask something of you one day, Rider, or your mate, and if I do, you will grant it." She spoke directly to Scarlet this time, who met her eyes and nodded in agreement.

With a flash the Raven disappeared, and Scarlet sat back into the chair with a slump. "Are they always like that?"

"Yes, for as long as I can remember."

"How often do they take human form?"

"Only when called."

"Is that what you did there? Called her to human form?"

"Yes."

Tyr had never before called one of his father's Ravens, and he was sure he would hear about it soon enough, once Muninn told the All Father about the desired message. Odin wouldn't like them messing with Ragnarok. Technically it was Scarlet, and Odin had no influence over the Riders. But Tyr would hear about it regardless.

"What did you write?" he asked as he cleaned up the ash the feather had left in the sink and tossed the paper towel into the garbage.

"I asked him to come back and meet us. Well, I guess me. I would prefer you not be there."

Tyr nodded. He didn't like the thought of her meeting the hellhound alone, but he also didn't want to face his slayer two times in under twenty-four hours.

Scarlet crossed the room, and he folded her in his arms dropping his cheek down to rest against the top of her head. She smelled like home, like life, like his life. He wanted her more than ever, and yet he wanted her to be happy and comfortable, only what she wanted to be. It was such a convoluted emotion to explain. So many ways to look at their love, and so many lenses to corrupt something so pure.

If he died, then it truly was the end of days meaning Scarlet would also have duties to perform. At least she wouldn't be left alone. But the thought of losing her with all that passion and fire and drive created a dull ache in his chest he didn't want to think about too hard.

In that moment he held her, and they were fine. He would focus on that. He might even succeed at it for a time if he didn't think about the doom and gloom of the last few days and remembered the time they'd spent together.

Five minutes of them gently holding each other passed and the phone rang announcing the arrival of a guest.

"It has to be Garmr," she said. "I'll be back as soon as it is done."

"Be careful and don't do anything foolish."

She nodded and kissed him hard on the lips before leaving the room. His heart somehow climbed up his chest and into his throat. Tyr stood alone in the room with nothing to do but wait.

Chapter Fifteen

Scarlet entered the bar and found the hellhound sitting at a high top table in the corner clutching a tall glass. He looked even more menacing with the shadows from the bar cloaking him in random darkness. The look on his face would scare away most humans, but as she climbed into the seat next to him he gave her a wide, toothy smile that was more creepy than comforting.

"I got your message, and I'm intrigued, especially at your messenger. We tried to catch the pretty one, but she slipped away too quickly. But we will continue to hunt."

Scarlet swallowed and hoped the Raven stayed out of harm's way. No doubt if something happened to her, others would be punished including her and Tyr.

"I just think that you and Tyr should go back to your original understanding," she said as a waiter came over to offer her a menu. She waved him away, and he retreated quickly.

"You act like I have a choice in the matter."

"Does Hel control you all by force? I thought you were merely following her since she controls your home. You followed Hades once too."

"Yes, but he abandoned us. And Hel is less—"he stopped and tasted a word in his mouth moving his lips around as if he swished a beverage"—forgiving."

Scarlet could only imagine the horrors they faced at Hel's beck and call. "You could come here to Earth and partner with us. Refuse to join the end of days and live life."

"As what? A human? You all look like humans that sometimes change to Riders. We are hounds that sometimes look human. We wouldn't fit in here; we wouldn't have a place."

The scent of sulfur around him grew stronger with his anger. Scarlet racked her brain to try and think of a way to get him to go along with her plan. If Hel controlled them, they were screwed. "Is there a way to break Hel's control? Of you, I mean," Scarlet asked.

"If she died, but there needs to be a ruler in the Underworld. Hel was second choice after Hades abandoned us, and that's who we're stuck with."

Scarlet slapped her palm on the table drawing the gazes of some of the nearest humans. "Ok, let's get this straight. Hades didn't abandon you. He's stuck in this just as much as the rest of us are. He had no choice."

"What do you mean?"

Scarlet already revealed too much. "I can't say as I'm compelled to silence by my companions, but Hades did *not* relinquish his throne by choice. You had to have seen the battle Hel waged against him and his subsequent torture at her hand. We freed Hades from torment."

Garmr looked into the water of his glass and licked his too wide lips. "Well, Hades is welcome to return to us. He simply needs to kill Hel and take her place."

"He can't."

"So he is still compelled to your side then?"

"He is still something to our side. I have no idea what."

The hound pursed his lips and stared at her with huge brown eyes. They might have been pleasant eyes if it were not for the hellhound part of him staring back at her.

"Then I guess that's it," she said shifting to slide off the high seat.

He nodded his head. "I don't want to die as much as your mate. Kill Hel and the original agreement stands. We can avoid each other again."

"Thank you for coming." She left with the imprint of his eyes on her back and the smell of sulfur clinging to her sweater.

The second she entered the hotel room Tyr seized her. "What did he say?"

"Calm down." Scarlet gripped his hand clutching her upper arm. "Sit down." She led him to the couch, and they sat into the plush cushions. "Basically, we're screwed."

"Screwed how?"

"He has no control. Hel commands them. He says that if we kill Hel, then they can resume the natural order of things, and he will leave you in peace. He seemed genuine."

Tyr slumped forward with his head in his palm, his other arm supporting the other side at the wrist. "I'm not afraid of him. Or to die. I would prefer to find another way if there is one."

She rubbed his back softly. "I know, love. I know." It was the same for her. If she could figure out a way to save everyone, she would. No one in their group, in the family, was disposable. Scarlet made her decision before he sat up and leaned in to kiss her.

"I love you," he whispered.

Scarlet smiled and kissed him back. It was because she loved him she would do this. He could go into the Underworld for her, and she would do the same. Besides, she was War. She had her sword. It was highly unlikely anyone would mess with her. She thought about it for a moment and decided she would call the Red Horse if need be as well. It would scare the shit out of anyone who saw her if she wasn't careful, but he could get her out of severe trouble.

The plan formed unbidden in her mind, and she would pursue it after he fell asleep so he wouldn't know. This way she could solve everyone's problems with one single stroke. Scarlet didn't mind taking the bitch's life for what she had done to Hades alone.

Luckily the hellhounds escorted her directly to Hel only a short time ago so she should be able to get to her easily if the boatman was available. She wondered if he followed a time schedule like the local bus route. The image of the dead sitting at a bus stop on the edge of the River Styxx came to mind, and she snorted in laughter.

"What is it?" he asked infected with her smile.

"I was thinking about the dead waiting for the boatman on the edge of the River Styxx like they would at a bus stop waiting for the bus." Saying it aloud was even better and soon she was dissolved into laughter, tears pooling at the corner of her eyes. Tyr stared at her, but she couldn't help it. The imagery was funny. Maybe he didn't think so because he'd never waited for the bus or worried about the sanitization of the bars to hold onto while riding.

"I guess it must be like that," he said. "But I don't understand why it is so hilarious."

She finally sat up wiping away the tears. "You've never ridden a bus before so you have no idea why it's so hilarious."

"Well, you will have to take me."

"On a bus?"

"Yes."

"Why would you want to ride a bus?"

"Because you seem so affected by it."

"No, it was terrible. If I could catch a communicable disease, I don't think I would have ever dared." She shook her head and took his hand to kiss the back of it. "Just forget it. How about you order us dinner and then we can play a game?"

A light entered his eyes. Scarlet knew how much he loved games. And this one he was bound to enjoy as it had long been one of their mutual favorites.

"Done," he said before planting a small kiss on her cheek. He left to order dinner, and her smile fell away as she thought about what she needed to do.

Chapter Sixteen

Tyr practically bounced as he watched her finish her dinner. If she wanted to play the game she was thinking of, then the night was young.

"Will you stop looking at me like that?" Scarlet grumbled before putting the last bit of food in her mouth. He whisked the plate away and came back to pull her into his arms. She laughed at his fervor, but he wasn't going to relent. He reached down and cupped her ass to lift her up. She wrapped her legs around his waist so he could support her other side with his arm.

There were many things Scarlet doubted in the world. The cleanliness of public restrooms, the reliability of politicians, and especially the actual heath characteristics of so called *health foods*. But that she would come back to Tyr wasn't one of her doubts. As he tightened his grip on her ass, she dragged her mind from the task ahead and fixed it on the sensation of his lips on hers and the hard muscles of his shoulders bunching under her hands.

"So tell me, love, what game did you want to play tonight?" he whispered in her hair before trailing his lips down her throat ending in a small bite.

Her insides were already liquid, but when his mouth touched the sensitive skin of her neck, she went molten. She barely held the capacity to begin the game let alone do her work later.

"You have to let me down." He released her with one last kiss. Scarlet went to the mini bar and grabbed some bottles and shot glasses. "Now get naked."

He laughed but did as he bid and stripped bare. Her mouth watered and her heartbeat sped up looking at him. He had a confidence that said he didn't have a care in the world. There wasn't a single day she hadn't see him naked when they were together in Asgard. He was completely unabashed in his nudity, and she loved that about him. When he'd learned the effect this had on her, he made sure to torture her at every available opportunity.

She stared at him too long and the next thing she knew he had her in the air and then on the bed with him naked between her still clothed legs. In true deity fashion he took what he wanted, when he wanted it, and she needed to stop letting him distract her. "Stop."

Tyr dropped his head onto her collarbone sending a jolt through her as the nerves collided. He reluctantly rolled off her and onto his back next to her, his erection jutting straight up in the air.

Scarlet sat up, grabbed a bottle, and poured a shot tossing it back before she lost her resolve. Something she happened to have plenty of on a regular basis, but tonight seemed to be lacking. She poured another shot and handed it to him. He sat up to take it while she poured a couple more shots and set them on the bedside table. After she did, Scarlet quickly undressed.

"That is more like it," he said moving to get up.

"No, stay."

Grumbling, he sat down as she climbed up beside him and lay down.

"Go get the shots."

She directed him to hand them to her one at time. First she placed one between her knees, the second at the plushest part of her thighs, and placed the final one right at the base of her sex. He watched with one eyebrow raised but said nothing.

"Now do the shots." She instructed him.

When he reached out to grab the first one she clucked at him. "No, no hands."

"I don't even get a handicap?"

Scarlet laughed against her will. "No, and I'll kick you for that later."

He sat down next to her hip and stared at the shots. Tyr maneuvered so he straddled her shins and then scooted so his butt jutted in the air as he put his face by her knees. He made the first shot look easy as he gripped it with his teeth, pulled it out, and then tossed it back in one gulp. Afterwards he tossed the glass onto a nearby chair and stared at the second shot. It was pushed further down so the top of the glass was level with her flesh. He dove in for that one and eventually was able to grip it with his teeth. His beard brushed her thigh, and she tried to keep from laughing at the tickling sensation. The third shot would be the most difficult.

"Don't spill," she said with mock innocence.

He bit her thigh hard enough to make her cry out before pushing his face to her center. Every nerve ending in that area tightened, and she took deep breaths to keep from running her fingers into his hair and having him forget about the shot. Finally he sucked it out from between her legs and tossed it back.

"My turn." He growled tossing the shot glass away. She swallowed as he pushed her up onto the pillows and used the space at the end of the bed to lay down so his face was directly at her core. He had been in this position before, and every single time he made sure she finished twice before he moved on.

She swallowed and reached out to grip the comforter as he slid his hot tongue between her legs dragging across every sensitive place. He knew her desires well enough to know exactly how to torture and tease her into a puddle of submission.

When he reached up, cupped the side of her hip, and dug his nails into the area above her hip bone, she spread her legs allowing him better access. The tiny edge of pain he provided allowed her something to cling to as he licked her repeatedly drawing out all kinds of sounds she hadn't even realized she was capable of creating. As she crested her first peak, she ground her hips up into his face.

Before she slipped over, he pulled back breaking all physical contact with her. He loved to torture her that way. The one moment she needed everything, he ripped it away and pulling her back away from her climax.

"Please." She begged.

"My dear, I don't plan to get you off with my lips tonight. This night, I'll use my cock to make you come, and then I'll do it again and again until I'm satisfied that you're satisfied."

His confession left her speechless. He climbed up so his face was level with hers and then positioned his hips, clutched himself, and then shoved himself inside her with one hard thrust. As his width stretched her, she cried out. Already so close to orgasm, she could barely hold on.

"Come for me, but know it will not be the last time." He pulled out and then surged forward again. It broke her. She shattered gripping his shoulders and dragging her nails across his flesh. Her orgasm triggered something in him or maybe it was the marking of his flesh, but he didn't remain quiet or gentle. He reared away and slammed into her over and over until she clutched him with her legs and hands and arms to keep from being shaken senseless. As soon as she came down from the first orgasm, she rode the wave up onto another. When he pressed his teeth into the top of her shoulder, she tumbled over again with great gasps.

To her surprise he followed slamming into her a few more times before groaning against her neck. She was sticky with sweat and liquor and his saliva, but she'd never felt better as he collapsed his weight onto her and lay his head between her breasts. Scarlet pulled his hair away from his temple and patted it gently enjoying the way the strands slid through her fingers. Scarlet wanted to fall asleep like that, curled up in his arms, but she didn't dare. If she slept, she couldn't guarantee she would be able to wake up and leave him.

After a few moments, his soft snore made her smile. She shifted his body off of her and placed a pillow under his head before climbing out of the bed and going to the bathroom. She dressed quickly and efficiently.

Scarlet had never undertaken a mission like this. Yes, she'd fought in battles against other immortals doing stupid things, but this was different. She had to be covert, and above all else no one could discover her intent, at least not until it was over. She grabbed the pen/sword and exited the room quietly. A sense of relief enveloped her when he didn't rush out of the room to follow her.

As she exited the hotel, Scarlet went to the nearest alleyway and called a door into the Underworld. To her surprise, no hellhounds greeted her. Maybe they wanted to wait and see what the outcome would be.

The trip the Underworld seemed easier than she expected. After she found the correct alleyway the hellhound used earlier and slid through to the other side, it didn't take any time to find the boatman. She could feel Charon's cold glare as he ferried her across. She wondered if the living were harder to ferry than the actual dead.

Once she was safely across the river, she followed the path into the palace. Scarlet had no way of telling whether it was night or day. She entered the palace slowly watching for any sign of hellhound or deity. She wasn't a god, but she wasn't mortal either. Being the embodiment of War had its advantages. Scarlet was sure if it came to a fight then she would win, but she had no way of knowing what sort of things Hel could access. Monsters, demons, random breakfast foods...no idea what the woman would throw at her.

The plan had seemed like a good one sitting safely back at the bar. Doubts crept into her mind. If Tyr woke up and found her gone, would he assume she ran away again? And what if her friends couldn't find her? What if she died in the Underworld and not a single person knew it? Scarlet wasn't entirely sure she could die. She'd taken a spear to the belly once and recovered from that.

The halls of the Underworld were as quiet as the dead. She laughed at her own cleverness in an attempt to push away the doubt. Finally she heard sound coming from a room and peered through the partially open door to find Hel putting lotion on her legs.

Scarlet hadn't thought this far ahead. What if she got in? What if she got this far? Should she wait until Hel fell asleep and kill her then? Or should she face her in hand-to-hand combat? She cursed herself for allowing Tyr to distract her enough that even her half-baked plan was half-baked.

She watched Hel finish her bedtime routine and climb into a large, ornate bed carved from Onyx. Hel snuggled under the covers, and Scarlet actually felt a little sorry for the woman. Until Tyr came to her mind and she remembered how the woman had sicced one of her henchmen on her husband. The guilt and pity evaporated, and she focused her mind to the task. Once Hel fell asleep, she would take her life and slip back home with no one the wiser.

Chapter Seventeen

Tyr woke with a jolt and glanced around at the silent room. Something was wrong. He couldn't quite put his finger on it because of the deep throbbing in his brain. The liquor had been stronger than he'd thought. Four shots in less than ten minutes had been a bad idea, even for a god.

"Scarlet," he called reaching out to the empty bed. *Cold.* He got up but squinted so any invading light wouldn't spear through his brain. The bathroom was empty as were all the rooms. He swallowed the ache building in his chest as he remembered a very similar situation.

Instead of succumbing to the rage beginning to boil in his belly, he picked up the phone and called her cell. Straight to voicemail. He dialed Cloris. She answered with a groggy hello.

"Cloris, is Scarlet with you?" He measured each word carefully, trying to remain calm when every nerve in his body screamed against the calm.

"No, she's not. Why, what's up?"

He took deep breaths in an attempt to remain calm. "She is not here." Hopefully those words were enough to get his point across.

"We'll be right over."

Tyr sat down on the bed and tried Scarlet's cell phone again. Then he remembered the pen. He teetered through the room looking for Scarlet's sword but found nothing. She also hadn't taken any clothes or belongings.

He sat down on the floor trying to figure out what was happening. If she ran away from him again, why didn't she take clothing? She took her sword and her phone, but why not her other belongings? He didn't know how long he sat there until the bell interrupted him. He dove for the door and tore it open. Cloris, Kat, Bianca, and Hades all stood on the other side.

"Honey, put some clothes on," Cloris said as Bianca spun around to stare at the opposite wall.

They trooped in the open door as he went in search of pants. He dressed sloppy and quick, not even sure if the clothes were clean or dirty. *Black t-shirt and blue jeans seem a fine pairing on the last night of your life.*

"Have you heard anything else? Tried her cell phone"?" Kat asked glancing around the disassembled room.

"No, and yes, I tried it a few times," he said. "What's the plan?"

"She wouldn't leave you," Bianca said. The woman saw too much of him, and it made him very uncomfortable. Since he'd first met her it was like she'd stripped his soul to its core and found it wanting. And yet they had a clairvoyant in their midst and weren't using her. "Seer, can't you divine where she is or something?"

"No, it doesn't work like that," Bianca replied.

"I don't know what to think. All I know is this is the same feeling I had before. The same empty, itching ache for her I had the last time she left. I see you all here and know she would leave me for you guys, but I cannot picture her leaving all of us."

"I know you're scared," Cloris said running her hand up his bare arm. "We'll find her. She wouldn't leave like this, not for any reason."

Tyr took a deep breath. "The hellhound."

"What about him?"

"Maybe he took her? Maybe he lured her out somehow? They spoke earlier at the bar for about twenty minutes. She didn't want me there, and when she got back she didn't go into much detail about what they'd talked about or what the plan was."

"We would smell it in the room. Cloris and Hades have a nose for that particular scent," Kat said.

"I can check something," Cloris said before disappearing.

Tyr stumbled back from the space where she used to be and looked at the others.

"She usually doesn't just disappear like that," Hades said by way of an apology.

A few moments later Cloris returned. "She's in the Underworld."

"What?" Tyr said. "That fucking hellhound must have said something to her or told her something. That is the only reason she would go there, alone for that matter." "Well," Tyr said as he grabbed his jacket off the nearby couch. "Let's go."

"Hold up, cowboy." Bianca snatched the back of his coat and held him back.

He could have ripped out of her grip easily, but he turned back and glared at her. "My wife could be hurt, in trouble, even dying, and you want me to wait?"

Bianca shook her head. "First off, drama queen, she isn't dying because we can't die until after the end of the world. Secondly, cool it because we're going to help you."

Something eased in Tyr as her words sunk in. "What can we do?"

"We can work together," Hades added.

Tyr wasn't sold on this plan. "You can't go down there. You know damn well that crazy bitch wants you most of all."

Hades shrugged. "My friend needs me. Besides I still have some pull down there. Or, well, I think I do."

Cloris headed out the door, and they all followed. "I have a quicker way, if you don't mind," she said reaching her arm out. They all placed a hand on her arms, hands, and shoulders. Tyr held his breath. One minute he'd been staring at the hotel door and the next he was staring at the black palace of the Underworld.

Hades let out an unintelligible sound but reached out took Cloris' hand. It was the first time he'd seen them show any sort of sympathy toward one another. It was strange, like seeing your parents kiss...not that his had done in a millennia or so.

"Let's go," Cloris said as they paraded up the broad stone steps into the palace. The empty halls surprised them as the palace normally crawled with hellhounds.

"Where is everyone?" Tyr asked. They entered the throne room and found Scarlet unconscious on the floor with a lone hellhound sitting over her. He was in dog form holding her wrist in his mouth.

The sight sent Tyr into a fury. There was no way he would allow her to suffer the same fate he would. He would rather die. "Back away from her, beast, or I'll rip your head from your body and use your entrails for a scarf."

The hound growled low, tightening his grip on her arm. Tyr saw red and dove toward them. He slid on his knees across the polished stone until he brushed the side of Scarlet's body. He saw the rise and fall of her chest. *She's unconscious, not dead. Why would she do something like this?* "What did you do hound? Speak!"

A feminine voice broke in. "Oh, she tried to kill me. You're lucky you have something I want or her head would be on a pike at the gates." Her voice travelled across the crowd. "Ah Hades, you came back to me."

"No, I haven't, Hel. I've only come to retrieve my friend."

She clutched her chest in mock pain. "You wound me, my love."

Hades remained silent. Tyr moved closer to the group as ghostly figures crowded around them. More specifically crowded around Hades. Some reached out to touch him, but he speared them with a glare and they retreated a respectable distance.

"Release her," Tyr said staring at the hound who held his wife.

Hades chuckled drawing everyone's eye. "Why, Hel, you're more clever than I ever gave you credit for. Really, I didn't think you could ever come up with a plan as clever as this. You get the dog to pretend to be on our side, lure Scarlet here knowing she would do anything to save the man she loves, and then set the trap as everything falls into place." He gave her a mock bow which she accepted with a nod of her head.

"To be honest I have always been quite clever, but because I'm not particularly beautiful people seem to overlook that quality. This was rather easy to be honest. I would not have had to do anything if you would have come of your volition. I don't particularly enjoy being the bad guy, but what is done is done." Hel stood, walked over to the hound holding Scarlet, and pet him on the head. The dog nuzzled her fingers as everyone looked on disgusted.

"Name your terms, woman, so I can have my wife back."

Hel continued her caresses as she spoke. "Simple. Hades stays, everyone else goes."

Cloris stepped forward, the souls skirting her as though she were contaminated with the plague. "It's not simple, and it won't happen. You may be queen in the Underworld, but I'm Death."

She said it conversationally, but goose bumps climbed Tyr's arms. He never wanted to get on that woman's bad side. Cloris shook her head and blackness covered her from head to toe, a black cape complete with hood, the traditional garb of death.

"You have no power over me. I'm immortal."

Death stepped forward, an otherworldly voice taking over her usually sweet and sultry tone. "Nothing is immortal. It is only a matter of finding the invitation."

"This is my realm, Rider," Hel said curling her lip in disgust. "You have no power over the dead here, and you have no power over me."

"But there is one here who died but still lives..." Death pointed a curtain off to the side.

Hel jerked forward as if she would attack Death but stopped herself in the next moment, her skirts swirling violently. "You wouldn't. That would be defying the All Father himself."

"The All Father is not my father nor my commander. I would take that life if you take my friend's. Ragnarok is not here now, but if you declare war on the Riders, there will be a war. And you will lose."

Bianca interrupted. "She has already decided. She will sacrifice even Baldir for Hades."

The hound growled drawing everyone's attention back to Tyr and Scarlet.

"Release her," Death commanded.

"Fine, but I'll take my bounty." Hel said waving a hand at the hound. It dropped Scarlet's arm but lunged for Tyr who was caught off guard by Scarlet's release.

He twisted to keep the snapping jaws of the hound's face away from his. The hound rolled across the stone floor in a flurry of fur and pointed teeth. The dog had an advantage as he had many more limbs, but Tyr had his strength. He held the dog's neck away with his hand until he found the other hellhounds circling him. They crept closer. Tyr stood still holding the hound by the neck away from him. One hound leapt on his back. He released the other to pry the new assailant's jaws from his shoulder.

The hounds descended on him in growls. A sound blasted through the hall, cracking like lightning minus the actual bolt, and everything went dark. The last thought in his mind was of Scarlet. That even if he died, the others could save her. At least she would be safe.

Chapter Eighteen

Scarlet woke to the sound of growling and snapping teeth. She bolted upright and crouched low. To her horror, she saw the others watching as Tyr was mauled to death by hellhounds. Moving on instinct, she reached into her pocket to pull out her sword and found a pen. An ordinary looking pen. Scarlet launched herself toward the fight, but Hades gripped her around the waist and pulled her back.

"Hades, if you don't let me go, I'm going to rip off your balls and feed them to you."

"He made me promise if it came to this, I would keep you safe. It was his wish, and I made an oath," he whispered in her ear.

Scarlet struggled, but he held her tight. He had the advantage of god-like strength. "Let me go." She growled clawing his arm in an attempt to rip herself from his grasp. But it was too late.

The hounds backed away, and Tyr lay in a bloody heap on the stone. Hades finally released her, and she ran to her husband's side. She pressed her forehead to his lifeless chest and cried. Not the lonely tears of the sad, but the deep gut wrenching wails of the grief stricken.

She dug her hands into his shirt, the blood and hounds' saliva sticking to her. The calm slowly descended and washed over her like a wave. She sat back on her shins and looked toward Hel. The hounds had killed her husband, but it was Hel who bore responsibility for his death. She stood leisurely and walked toward Hel, who didn't even have the good sense to look frightened.

The hounds growled in warning as she drew closer. They could growl, attack, and rip her to shreds, but she didn't care. Nothing mattered except the warm gush of Hel's blood on her hands. No matter how it happened.

She closed the distance in a few short strides and grabbed Hel by the neck. The woman was taller and a goddess so she retained an advantage, but Scarlet had her own edge. A madness crept in, and if she Hel hadn't taken her sword, she would break the seal and doom them all. If only to take the crazy bitch down.

The goddess pulled her hands away easily with one of her own and smiled down at Scarlet. "Ah, Rider, you're no match for me."

"Give me back my sword, and I'll show you."

"This?" A voice said from behind her.

She turned to find Garmr naked, wearing the blood of her husband, clutching her pen in his hand. The rage replaced the madness, and she charged him. To his credit he stood his ground as she slammed into him knocking him down.

"Why are not you dead?" she screamed as she straddled his stomach and battered his face with her hands. She slapped and punched and all out thrashed him, until Cloris pulled her off. At the woman's touch Scarlet calmed, and as Cloris' arms wrapped around her, hard as a vice, she succumbed to the promised tranquility.

Scarlet woke up in her hotel room with the others staring down at her. Rage still poured through her, and she screamed. She lay in the middle of the room she shared with Tyr and screamed until she panted to draw breath. Once she stopped, the silence rang in her ears.

She sat up and glared at Hades. "If we did not need you, I would kill you."

He looked at her calmly. "I know."

"We need to get the sword back." Cloris eyed Scarlet with a wary look.

"Stop looking at me like that," she snapped finally standing on wobbly legs.

"How did they get the drop on you? You're the best fighter of all of us."

"They drugged me. The dog's mouths were laced with some sort of poison. It knocks you out cold. I remember sneaking up to Hel's door. I turned to find a hound, and then nothing until I woke up." The memories swamped her. The vision of Tyr's broken body on the black stone, imprinted on her mind. She shook it away when the urge to scream surged inside of her again. "What do you want to do?"

"It's simple," Hades said. "I have to trade myself."

"One seal for another is not a good trade," Cloris added.

"Yes, but the sword can't try to escape on its own, can it?"

"Hades, it's not an acceptable trade," Cloris said gently gripping his hand.

He pulled it back and shook his head. "Then what do you propose?"

Cloris took a deep breath. "I don't know. I suppose you're really the only thing that madwoman wants, but I still don't think it is a good idea."

"You never think anything I come up with is a good idea." Hades moved into Cloris' space and shocked Scarlet to her bones when he planted a rough kiss against her friend's lips. Cloris returned the kiss and frowned. "You just don't want to lose me," he said gently.

Cloris caressed his lower lip with her index finger. "You're right. I don't."

Anger welled up in Scarlet again. No one wanted to sacrifice Hades, but Tyr was certainly a fitting sacrifice for absolutely nothing.

Bianca came up beside her and took her hand in a hard grip before whispering to her. "He didn't sacrifice himself for nothing. He sacrificed himself for you."

That hit her hard. If she'd never left, if she'd waited and developed a plan with them all, he wouldn't have gone there to find her. He wouldn't have been so reckless. The truth crashed around her sending her to her knees, and Bianca stepped away.

"What did you say?" Cloris asked as Bianca knelt down beside Scarlet.

"The truth."

"What truth?" Cloris demanded.

"That Tyr sacrificed himself. She took it upon herself to think no one cared and that Tyr's sacrifice meant nothing."

Cloris pursed her lips but said nothing as she touched Scarlet's face. "Tyr's sacrifice was for you, yes, but he would make that choice every single time it was presented to him. He would give anything for you as he showed. He loved you, and you need to accept that fighting for you was his choice."

Scarlet swallowed and the tears began to flow again. Cloris held her, the skin of her collarbone chilled, but it felt good against Scarlet's hot cheeks.

"What do you want me to do?" A new voice entered the room.

Scarlet looked up at the man who all but glowed as he buttoned his pants. His skin was a sun-kissed brown, and he had blonde ringlets framing his perfect face. He almost rivaled Hades for beauty, but his was warm and attainable whereas Hades was cold and unapproachable.

"For fucks sake, do we need any more harbingers of the apocalypse in one room?" Bianca groaned before plopping onto the bed.

He glared at her and bowed to Cloris. "Thank you, Lady Death, for saving me from Hel." He eyed Hades with a look of mutual understanding.

"Baldir, please just sit for now," Cloris said still trying to comfort Scarlet.

It all sounded far away as if she couldn't possibly be living this moment. The memory, pain, and anger all a distant vision outside herself.

"Well, this is simple," Scarlet said jumping up. "We trade the sun god for my seal and the remains of my husband." She had finally mastered herself, shoving everything deep inside to deal with later. It wasn't an ideal situation, but neither was losing your husband after a Lone Ranger episode.

"I'll not return to that place," Baldir interjected as he strode toward the couch.

Cloris glared at him, and he actually flinched. "Sit down and shut up. If you don't do as I say, I'll show you I can be an even crueler mistress than Hel." Her eyes blazed with a fire Scarlet had never seen before. She'd never seen her friend this emotionally upset and riled. If she didn't know any better, she would think Cloris cared about what happened to Tyr.

"Honey," Cloris said as she turned to her again. "We can't trade Baldir for the seal, the main reason being its cruel, and the second reason being, he would rather die than return to her side."

"There seems to be a lot of that going around." Scarlet turned toward Hades. "What did she do to you?"

Hades turned to her with an icy stare. "That is none of your concern."

"No, really. I need to know what I'm asking of you. What you're sacrificing in order to get the seal back."

He sighed heavily and shifted against the wall so he could hide his face. Cloris walked around Scarlet and approached Hades cupping his shoulders as if to offer support.

"When Hel started her siege against me in the Underworld, no other deities were willing to help. I fought her alone, which was entirely unprecedented because had Zeus been attacked you'd better believe the entire pantheon and the void would have been called forth to protect him. Anyway, she took me as a war criminal, and there are no laws about the treatment of war criminals. She handcuffed me to the bed with an Agate pendant wrapped around my neck so tight it cut into my skin." Scarlet watched him rub his neck as if the memory still plagued him.

After a moment he continued. "She did unspeakable things to me. Calling me her plaything. The most beautiful god in existence reduced to her toy. She raped me, used me until the power of the

Revelations prophecy became enough to drag me from her bed to Cloris' side. I don't know if you recall my first day with you?" Hades asked turning once more to face Scarlet, a fine sheen of moisture coating his eyes.

Scarlet wracked her brain. They weren't born they were created to await a prophecy some two thousand years or so in the future. When Hades had arrived he looked like a half-starved scarecrow, but somehow remained stunningly beautiful. A beauty becoming more apparent the more he grew comfortable with them. "I sort of remember." Scarlet hedged.

"Well, the day I was surrounded by you all, I expected further punishment, degradation, and torture. When you treated me like any other person, I began to grow more secure, but I have never fully trusted another woman until Cloris showed me a different way." He reached down and held her hand before kissing it gently on the knuckle.

"So basically you're willing to go back to that torture for us to get the seal back? How is that worth it?"

"Not just for the seal, but for Tyr too. I came to like him. You two complement each other. Also because if the seals are broken, then this little family I have that has offered me so much when I wasn't willing to even listen will be destroyed. I can't live with that if I have something I can offer in exchange."

"How are you okay with this?" Scarlet asked Cloris.

"Oh, I'm not. I fully intend to show Hel what kind of power Death has over the ruler of the Underworld. I haven't decided if I should do it before or after I rip her throat out with my scythe."

Bianca was of course the one who giggled. "Not to take the severity out of the situation here but, you have a scythe?"

"It's kind of part of the job, but I don't always use it." Scarlet waited, and Cloris sighed. "I only use it when I need to scare people. Some souls are, well, sticky, they don't want to leave or think they can bargain with me, but when I pull the sucker out they seem to listen."

Hades cleared his throat. "Can we get back to the matter at hand, ladies? I don't want to go down there blind. We need a plan."

"No amount of planning can account for variables," Scarlet said.

Hades nodded his agreement. "I guess you would be the expert on strategy. Or would that be Bianca?"

Bianca chuckled. "We agree to disagree on that point."

"We could use you to see for us. Try and feel out if we need to alter plans to create something else altogether," Scarlet said switching into War mode.

"Well, what is the plan?" Bianca crossed her arms under her small breasts.

"Trade Hades for Tyr and the sword." Immediately pity entered Bianca's eyes, and Scarlet looked away to avoid it.

"Well, that doesn't seem like much of a plan, more of a surrender." Bianca pointed out.

Scarlet shifted on her feet trying to keep from growing angry with Bianca for poking holes in the plan. "The thought being Hades could try to escape."

"Yes, but didn't he try before without success?" Bianca noted.

Scarlet tried again. "Well, maybe Hel won't consider him a war criminal now or maybe we could negotiate some provisions with his stay there."

"Cause Hel seems like the type to offer mercy."

Another point for Bianca. Scarlet sighed and shrugged. War mode fail.

For the first time Bianca looked up and noticed Baldir sitting on the couch opposite them. "Do you have anything to offer this conversation, sunshine?"

He glanced at Cloris who rolled her eyes. "Speak," she ordered him.

"Don't call me sunshine." Baldir glared at Bianca.

Cloris sighed in exasperation. "Anything else?"

"Other than she still employs the use of binding stones and humiliates her prisoners, no. The only thing that kept me remotely safe was that she feared retribution at Frigg's hand should she defile her son. She only stripped me naked and paraded me through the Underworld on her arm."

Scarlet watched as Bianca teetered slightly and then shook herself.

"Did you have a vision?" Scarlet asked.

Bianca nodded. "Nothing bearing on this situation though." She glanced back at Baldir with an almost malicious expression.

"Fine," Scarlet said as she began to pace. "We need a plan." She chanted in time with her steps, and everyone allowed her to ruminate.

Chapter Nineteen

The descent back into the Underworld felt more dramatic to Scarlet. They walked in heads held high, ready for a fight. Like last time she had been there, no hellhounds prowled the area. They may answer to Hel, but Cloris scared them and most creatures of the Underworld.

The palace, the paths, and everyone else looked the same. Nothing had changed, but Scarlet didn't feel the same. Nothing was the same without Tyr. Before, when they'd lived apart, at least she could think about him and consider what he might be doing to pass the time. If he'd found another lover or if he ever nailed the kick they'd once been trying to perfect together.

She couldn't imagine any of those things. He was gone, and nothing she could do would change that. If she thought about him, she would only weep because there was nothing to think about except his ashes spread across the ocean of Asgard.

What she couldn't figure out is why his parents hadn't come in an attempt to save him or at least seek revenge for their son's murder. Her only conclusion was they assumed the Ragnarok was upon them and they could not interfere. His and Garmr's prophecy was well known. Many in the void, Asgard, and all other realms would be hiding, fleeing, or preparing to play the role they themselves inhabit for the end of days.

For a moment Scarlet entertained the notion. The seal was out in the open, and Tyr dead. Maybe it was time for them and not even leaving the void could alter their destinies once they'd been decided.

The palace loomed before them, and Scarlet realized Cloris had been clutching her arm, guiding her along, as she lost herself in her thoughts. She shook herself to the present and gently pulled her arm from Cloris' grasp. Her friend gave her a small smile as they stepped up into the palace.

"I thought you'd be back," Hel said from the throne room.

They entered as a group, the tension almost palpable.

"You have some things that belong to us," Scarlet said, stepping forward to meet the intense gazes of the hellhounds as they circled their mistress.

Hel patted her arms and her upper thighs as if searching for something. "Oh? I don't believe so."

Scarlet curled her hands into fists ready to strike that way if need be. "You have my sword."

Hel pulled the pen from beside her on the throne. "This ol' thing? I thought it was nothing more than an ink pen. My hound must have been confused."

Scarlet glared at her. "You already know how I feel about games."

"Oh yes," she mocked. "Apparently you lose at them too often and now you dislike them. But my dear, when you enter the realms of the gods you better learn to enjoy games because gods live for them. They live for anything that will make the day more exciting. Usually those stupid little humans work nicely, but I have found myself upping the ante lately with you dear ones."

"What do you want me to say?" Scarlet asked opening her hands and turning around. "I don't have any weapons. I'm not here to play your game. I ask for my property and the remains of my husband, nothing more."

"What husband might that be?"

"My husband, Tyr. The man you viciously attacked with you mutts."

The closest hellhound growled, and Scarlet lost control bending down to growl in his face. "You know what your punishment will be, dog? War."

She grabbed his muzzle with her hands and looked into his black eyes before releasing him. Instantly he turned to his companion and bit its neck, and there it spread like a virus through the ranks of hounds. All save the one at Hel's right hand. She held his collar and refused to allow him to enter the fray.

"You seem to be playing games too, my dear," Hel said as she stood and dragged her hound along beside her. "Be still!" she shouted, and the animals stopped moving. Even in the throes of a fight, they all froze in place.

"That will need sorting later." Hel waved it away as if it meant nothing. "Now, what were you saying about this husband?"

Scarlet crossed her arms under her breasts and stood her ground against the approaching woman. She towered over her easily, but Scarlet didn't fear her because she had nothing else to lose.

That one touch of power surged under her skin begging to be used again, drawing her into its web of temptation. "I wouldn't come closer, bitch, because if you get within touching distance of me, I'll ruin your entire world. Hades may not have defeated you on his own before, but trust me, I can do it alone."

"But only if you touch me? Hmm, that is a limited power," Hel said stopping inches out of her reach.

Bianca stepped up. "She may need to touch you, but I don't."

Hel eyed her with a mix of apprehension and amusement. "I see you brought a child to fight beside you, how original."

"I'm no child." Bianca reached out to Hel and closed her fist. "I'm Conquest, and everything bows to my will."

Hel dropped to her knees and clutched at her throat. After a moment Bianca released her. The goddess fell forward on her hands taking deep racking breaths.

"I forgot how good that felt." Bianca shook out her hand. "Do I need to do it again?"

Hel rocked back and stood. Her faithful dog still by her side. "You come into my home and attack me?" She moved toward Bianca, but the girl put up her hand again. This time Hel stood battering an invisible wall.

"You thought because we don't flaunt our powers, don't abuse humans, or live in the void that somehow we are weak and useless. You forget that we are the Horsemen of the Apocalypse. We bring on the end of days, even the end of your days," Bianca said holding Hel back.

Scarlet sauntered forward. "With only two of us, we have ended your little game. Imagine the might of all of us united. Why, we might even be able to take back the Underworld and restore it to its rightful owner."

"You wouldn't dare." Hel struggled against the invisible prison Bianca created.

"Give us what we came for, and we will leave you in peace. But only if you leave us in peace. That being said, I don't know what the All Father is going to do to you once he finds out you murdered Tyr."

Bianca stepped up beside Scarlet, still blocking Hel from reaching her. "Hand over the pen," she said very clearly, and Hel's arm extended to drop it into Scarlet's hand.

"Thank you for your cooperation." Scarlet sneered. "We also need my husband's remains."

"What would you do if I fed them to my dogs?"

Scarlet felt her control slip at Hel's proclamation before she shook herself back into the present. "You wouldn't dare. If you deny a deity the chance at an afterlife, you doom yourself to the worst fates. You live here; you know what they are."

Bianca locked eyes with Hel and shook her head. "No, she won't reveal it, and I can't steal truth from a person's lips. It's beyond me."

Cloris approached and whispered in Scarlet's ear. "Let's get the sword home safely, and we will return for Tyr's remains. I'll go myself to the All Father and ask him to weigh in."

Scarlet pursed her lips so a string of profanities didn't escape. "Fine."

Bianca lowered her arm but spoke clearly to Hel. "You will not follow us, you will not send your dogs, or what is left of them, to follow us. Is that clear? Nod if you understand."

Hel nodded but not without spitting toward Bianca. "You will regret this, little pony. I'll see to it personally."

"Yeah...right," Bianca said before turning and leading the group from the palace.

Once they cleared the gate however, Scarlet knew something wasn't right. "This is not my sword."

Bianca reached out and took it. "Nope, nothing."

"Maybe I didn't feel it while we were in the midst of all that. Or Hel somehow replicated our magic," Scarlet said waving at the palace in general.

"Bianca, you lead the others home. Scarlet and I will return for her sword," Cloris said, already walking back up the black stone steps.

Scarlet followed and found Hel in the middle of her throne room laughing.

"Didn't get very far?" she asked sitting up and then standing.

Scarlet tossed the pen at her which Hel caught in mid-air and crunched in her hands before dropping the broken pieces to the ground. "Not losing your touch are you?"

"Give me my sword." Scarlet tried to remain calm. This woman had mocked them, murdered her husband, and basically threatened everything she stood for. She wouldn't be allowed to live long, and it would only be seconds if she kept toying with them.

"You want your sword, but I think there might be something you would be more interested in." Hel walked back to sit on her throne. She snapped her fingers and a figure in a hooded cloak came out from behind a curtain. Scarlet and Cloris turned to face it, unsure if this was another of the woman's tricks or not.

"Remove your hood, darling," Hel said. The figure stripped the cloak off letting it flutter to the floor.

Before her stood the broken and battered body of her husband Tyr. "How...?" Her mind skipped like a scratched record against a needle. "What is this? Another trick?"

"No trick, you left him here, half-dead. I just kept your garbage."

Scarlet rushed over and lifted his chin to meet her eyes. "Baby, talk to me."

He met her eyes, but they were not Tyr's. They were empty, his body only a shell. She swung back to Cloris. "Where is he?"

Cloris closed her eyes and turned up her palms as if she were awaiting a summer rain. After a few moments she twitched and opened her eyes. "He is in Elysium, and yet his body remains here."

Scarlet stalked up the dais toward Hel. "You're one manipulative bitch. Give me my sword," she said through clenched teeth. "If you don't, I'll set you on every deity within the realm until the All Father or Zeus or who-the-fuck-ever has to stretch forth his hand to stop you."

Hel placed the sword in her hand but smiled. "You might be surprised in your journey, however, because Helheim has finally descended."

"I should kill you now and save you the trouble of redecorating."

Hel only smiled at her, and Scarlet found that the most unnerving about the whole situation.

"I'll help you find him." Cloris led the way out of the palace.

A faint sheen of ice coated the stone of the palace and a strange wall formed off in the distance. Scarlet hadn't noticed it before because she hadn't been looking for it. Finally the sound of the River Styxx grew louder whereas before it flowed softly along. They walked toward it and found it roiling with heavy white rapids as ice clung to it is shores.

"It is a new world order. Hades is officially gone from this place. He must have denounced something in himself when he was here so the realm finally recognized it had a new ruler. Maybe that is what Hel sought all along."

"I can't say. That woman is trickier than a certain snake we've heard about." Scarlet looked around. "Which way to Elysium?"

Cloris pointed East, and they headed that way. The path before them stretched further than they could see, but the tread ground, the path clear from the tamped down Earth, led the way. They passed no errant souls wandering the plains or other areas.

"Aren't there usually things out here?" Scarlet asked.

"Souls you mean?"

"Yeah, I guess."

"Occasionally there are, but not always."

None of it felt right. She was on a quest to find and restore her husband's soul. How much more old world could this situation get? They walked for what felt like hours before Scarlet spoke up. "Why have we been walking so long? Can't you fly or something?"

Cloris laughed. "No, I can't fly, but I can disappear and appear at will."

"So, tclcport."

"We used too much power in the play with Bianca. I have a little left, but I want to save it in case it's needed."

"Never mind. So tell me, while we walk slowly along this path, what is up with you and Hades? I saw you guys kiss, but I have never seen you two be even remotely affectionate toward one another."

Cloris didn't immediately answer, and Scarlet worried she'd stepped over some sort of boundary she was meant to steer clear of.

"Well, it is sort of a long story."

Scarlet gestured to the vast empty landscape before them. "We might have some time."

"Well, Hades immediately hated me. As I could understand, he assumed I would be like Hel, yet another woman he was chained to and forced to obey. When I showed complete disinterest in him however, he took it as a personal affront to his looks."

"Men, right?"

"Finally, he asked me why I was so unattached to him or how I couldn't want to make him do things like Hel did." Cloris shuddered and crossed her arms to warm herself before continuing. "I told him that I wasn't unaffected, I just didn't think surface beauty was everything. Of course then he assumed I thought him shallow. This went on for about a thousand years until he walked in on me in bed with a lover. After that he acted like I didn't exist. When we finally came to Earth and he could sort of have a free will again, everything changed. We went from a strained, odd relationship to business partners and then to lovers. I don't really know how it happened. It's kind of recent but electrifying."

Scarlet smiled at her friend's happiness. "Maybe we will have another wedding soon; one you all can actually witness."

"Don't get ahead of yourself."

Scarlet grew hopeful. If her husband's body remained alive, maybe they could restore his soul and take him home.

They stepped up onto a field of men fighting. They battled intently slamming armor against armor. The residents of the field were all men, and they all wore armor and battle dress from Roman attire all the way to modern ACU's. Scarlet blinked trying to find Tyr. She did, after a while. He circled the edge of the field as if he monitored the group. She broke into a run at the sight of him.

"Tyr!" she yelled as she ran, but he didn't look up. "Tyr!" She got within a few feet of him, and his eyes opened wide.

"Scarlet, is that you? I never hoped to find you here. How did you get here? Why do you look so ashy?" A look seized him, and he dropped to his knees in the dust, swirling it around. "You died, and I wasn't there to help you."

"Tyr, can you hear me? I'm not dead."

He stared at her as if she were a ghost.

"Cloris, do something before I start having some sort of heart attack."

Cloris approached and looked at him. "It is part of the Underworld. He sees you as a ghost or a figment of his imagination perhaps. He can't hear you or touch you. He doesn't realize that he's dead."

"How is that fair?"

"You know the saying, 'Life isn't fair.' Well, neither is death."

"Can't you do something? I mean, you're physically Death."

"Yes, I'm Death, not life. He is already dead, what can I do?"

"How about ideas to fix him, got any of those?"

Cloris tapped her bottom lip in though. "Maybe one, but it's not a good idea. It might actually be worse than him being dead?"

"And, what is that?"

"You see that wall over there. I think it's Hel's wall. It restores the dead to life, but they have no memories of how they came to be there. Everything will be wiped away from before he even found you again. To him he will probably still be searching for you, or maybe you won't exist to him at all."

"So he would live, but we'd have to live without each other?"

Cloris nodded solemnly.

"Then he will live. Where is Jesus when you need him? He did this shit once, can't he show us how it works?"

"I don't think he frequents the Underworld."

Scarlet stared at Tyr, still kneeling in the dust.

"How do we get him to the wall?"

"Try to lead him there. He might follow you thinking he's following your soul."

Scarlet crouched down and waved for him to follow her. Thankfully it worked, and he rose up, wiped his face with a grimy arm, and followed her toward the wall. Cloris trailed behind. When they got to the wall they found it made of stone and completely impenetrable.

"They really don't want us to get through this thing?" She grasped the crevices between the stones.

"I can help, but only if you think it is what you want." Cloris gave her a pointed look.

"Yes, please, help me." Scarlet stared at Tyr who kept glancing between her and the wall.

"Then say goodbye. This may be the last time you see him. He could get all his memory of you wiped or only a little. There is no way to know."

Scarlet reached out to touch his face. A flash of memory. The first time she touched him in genuine love took her unawares. They'd been lying in his bed in Asgard, and he'd rolled over, naked as always, and whispered sweet things in Old Norse into her ear. Well, as far as she knew they were sweet, they sounded romantic, not bawdy. He'd pulled her close by her waist until he spooned her, and he'd kissed her neck, her cheeks, and even her eyelids as he spoke. It had seemed as if he almost spent that time worshipping her. She'd loved every second of it, and she'd pulled him to her lips, not to start sex but to show him exactly how she felt about him. To make him feel her love through that kiss. It was something she would never forget.

Tears sprang to her eyes, but she blinked them away before Cloris could see. "I love you. You're my heart and my world and there will never be another for me. I wish you happiness, even if it is not in my arms."

He couldn't hear her, but he could see her outstretched hand and knew she said something. "I love you," he whispered.

"Goodbye."

He disappeared with Cloris in a flash of light.

Chapter Twenty

Tyr woke with the worst headache of his life. He sat up in his bed in Asgard and stretched his arms over his head and then his fingers. It took a moment before it hit him. He had two arms, two hands, and ten fingers. He pulled them back down and stared at his hands. *How in the hell had that happened?* He tried to remember, to recall, what had taken place the previous night but there was nothing but an empty space and a scorching headache that promised to grow worse if he pressed it further.

He threw off the covers with his right hand, something he hadn't done in so long he laughed out loud at the novelty of it. He swung his legs over the side and stood, but something caught under his foot. Tyr reached down and picked it up. It was brown elastic forged in a circle. He flipped it around and back and forth trying to figure out where it came from. He had no reason to tie his hair at home. Even when he worked out, he used a thin rod to keep it away from his face.

Perhaps it belonged to a servant girl. He held it to his nose in hopes it might carry a scent he could remember. He had a very good nose for scents. Tyr inhaled deep the smell of vanilla. His heart beat faster, and he had to sit down from the onslaught of strange emotions. He reached up to find tears leaking from the corners of his eyes.

"What is this?" He stared at the tears sliding down his finger. Something was wrong. He felt wrong. His hand was returned to him, but he still felt a part of him missing. Like he wasn't entirely there.

He got back up and headed toward his kitchen only to trip over a punching bag at the end of his couch. One that definitely didn't belong to him. He never liked them. What use is an opponent who doesn't strike back?

He picked up the bag and stared at it. He could hear something pounding away at it, the squeak of the chains holding it aloft. All in his mind like an echo. "What is this?"

For a moment he considered Loki scheming again. Maybe the god of mischief found a way to give him his hand back only to take it away whenever he felt the urge. "Loki, if this is you, you'd better knock it off before I rip out your balls and feed them to you."

A voice startled him from behind. "Wow, you even curse alike. That is so strange. My name is Hades, and you've been resurrected."

Tyr stared at the man. How could he not? He was the singular most beautiful man he'd ever seen. "What do you want, and why are you in my house?"

"I came to help. You feel lost right now, as if something is missing and you can't quite put your finger on it? Right?"

Tyr didn't respond. He still suspected Loki's tricks, but he was incapable of making such alluring illusions, even if he held no attraction to men. "How do you know what I'm feeling or not feeling right now?"

Hades smiled wide. "What can I say? I'm an expert on this sort of thing."

"Oh? What sort of thing?"

"Death."

Tyr looked around his home. Had he somehow died and he not realized? He looked down at his restored hand. It would explain his returned extremity. "How did I die?"

"Well, you angered the current goddess of the Underworld, along with some of your friends, and well, she sicced her dogs on you."

"You mean...Garmr? But that means the end of days."

"Yeah, we haven't really gotten to that part yet, but we're working on it. Apparently since you're technically alive now and didn't die, the prophecy is still in effect. Like it took the entire situation into account. Who knows with fates?"

"So Garmr died too?"

"Um...I'm not sure, actually. I didn't check. But Scarlet did a number on the beasts after they attacked you."

"Scarlet?" The name struck him like the swoosh of a basketball in a net. Thor always liked to play the game: Tyr never understood it as he couldn't play with one hand.

"Ah, resonated huh?"

"Yes. Who is Scarlet?"

"Well, that would be better explained on Earth."

"Earth? Why Earth? Why would I go there?"

"Why on Earth?" Hades repeated the words before laughing out loud. He took in Tyr's expression and sobered with a few chuckles. "Never mind," he continued. "Do you want answers or not?"

Tyr stared at him. He had no way of knowing if this man could be trusted or not. He had no assurances as to his allegiances or anything. "Who are you?"

"I told you, I'm Hades."

"But that is simply your name not who you are."

Hades nodded. "Fair enough. I'm formerly god of the Underworld and currently a sort of sidekick to the Horsemen of Death."

"What does a sort-of-sidekick do?"

Hades laughed. "Anything his mistress asks of him. Now get dressed and hurry. I have someone you've been dying to meet."

Chapter Twenty-One

Scarlet paced back and forth in the hotel she had shared with Tyr. She could have gone back to her apartment, but this place still smelled like him. She refused to even allow them to take her bed sheets. Tyr would have said he paid them enough she could do whatever she wanted with the sheets.

She ran her hands over the folds of the red dress Bianca made her wear. It hugged her curves nicely but elicited a sense of self-consciousness. Red was a conspicuous color, and she didn't like to be conspicuous in any way.

Bianca rushed in the door and shouted, "he's here!"

Scarlet almost toppled over. Never had she been more discombobulated. All she could think about was that last look of longing on his face before Cloris took him away. After that, nothing was the same. She'd begun to get to know him again only to have him stolen away abruptly. It was unfair and downright cruel.

She reached up and touched the cluster of raised scabs on the side of her neck. The moment she'd found her way out of the Underworld she'd went straight to the All Father. He'd laughed at her. In her anger and rage, she challenged him to a fight. For a moment she thought he might take her up on it. He wouldn't be the first immortal curious about his or her might against the embodiment of War.

But he shook his head and sent his Ravens to attack her. The pair of them were fast and swooped in, gouging her neck before flying away. The All Father had then said, "Let that be a warning. Leave me and stop meddling in things that don't concern you."

Scarlet had left in a state of shock. She barely remembered getting back to the hotel room and curling up in the sheets to find his scent there. Afterward it took all her friends to drag her out of the bed to feed and bathe her before letting her rest again.

Finally, Cloris had enough and enlisted Hades' help to find Tyr and bring him to her, no matter the state he was in. But not before Cloris had carried her into the shower and hosed her down with icy water to get through to her. Scarlet had snapped out of the stupor in rage which Bianca easily controlled. Scarlet had vented her anger on herself, but minus a few bruises, she was fine.

The power they'd used in the Underworld still recharged so they weren't able to do much by way of magical ability. Bianca felt the worst since they'd returned. The power loomed like a drug over her head, a temptation she wanted desperately but shouldn't have.

Scarlet's mind snapped back to Tyr. There was no way to know his state and how he would react to her. A knock broke her pacing, and Bianca threw her a small bottle of liquor before retreating to the outer room. Scarlet tossed it back. The alcohol burned through her all the way to her belly.

Hades entered first, eyeing her carefully for any signs of crazy, she was sure. Then Tyr followed close behind looking everywhere as he entered. When no one jumped out at him, he walked into the room and stopped short when he saw her.

She held her breath, waiting for him to say something, anything, but he didn't speak.

He stared at her and then walked closer and sniffed her neck. He stepped back again. "Who are you?"

"I'm Scarlet."

His brows furrowed as he looked her up and down. Then she noticed his hand. He had two hands. She had never known him with both hands. Scarlet reached out to touch it, but he yanked it behind him and gave her a look full of suspicion.

"What is this? Another of Loki's schemes? Am I being punked?"

"Um...no. I'm afraid I don't know Loki."

His eyes softened slightly. "Well, if you knew him, you would not say that. It is probably a good thing."

Hearing his voice set her heart beating frantically and her body tingling. It was like the whole of her had fallen asleep, and she shook it out so that only a few lingering tingles remained. She decided to drop the bomb and see what happened. "I'm Scarlet. Your wife."

He laughed, long and loud. "I have never married. I have never even had an interest in marrying."

"Well, once upon a time you did, and then you died."

"Hades told me I died, but if I'm dead why am I not in Helheim or Valhalla? Or one of the other realms meant for the dead?"

"Well, you died when the worlds were sort of in transition, so you got some of the old regime and some of the new."

"I don't know what that means."

She led him to the table, and Hades disappeared the way Bianca went. "When we married you told me a story about a wild Viking tamed by a woman." His brow furrowed, but she pressed on reciting his favorite lines:

SPEAK! speak! thou fearful guest,
Who, with thy hollow breast
Still in rude armor drest,
Comest to daunt me!
Wrapt not in Eastern balms,
But with thy fleshless palms
Stretched, as if asking alms,
Why dost thou haunt me?

When she finished they both attempted to conceal the telltale sheen of tears in their eyes.

"My mother told me when I found the one I would tell her that story. Who are you that you would tame me?" he asked reaching out a hand for hers.

"I'm just me, and I think it was you who tamed me. I was lost before you came along with your quick wit and clever hand."

He laughed rubbing the pad of her thumb with his own. "I don't remember you. Why and how can't I remember you? Your scent and the resonance of your voice seems familiar. Even your name touches somcthing in my chest, but I can't quite understand what could have happened that I would not remember someone as lovely as you."

She smiled as a wet tear slid down her cheek. How far she had come from ice queen refusing to admit the defeat by showing a single tear, to a person who could cry openly in the arms of her beloved?

"How did we meet?" he asked, alternating between wiping his face and tilting his head back to stop more tears from flowing.

"Well, it is kind of a funny story. You told me that you could offer me more pleasure in a night than any man with two hands. I took you up on your challenge."

Tyr laughed. "You must have struck me then because I have never been so brazen in my life. How did it turn out? Did I rise to the challenge?"

"You did, admirably."

"Good." He clutched her other hand in his, and it felt perfect to hold both of his hands in hers, like his had never gone missing in the first place. "Tell me who you are, Scarlet."

"Well, that's a very long story. Maybe we could get something to eat, and I could tell it to you," she suggested. They could try the dating thing she'd heard so much about. Tyr swept her off her feet the first time, and she fully intended to do the same for him this time around. She watched him carefully as he gazed at their clasped fingers.

His voice wavered as he spoke. "You know you're the first woman I've ever been able to hold in both my hands? I was only a young man when I gave up my hand. I'd not yet known the touch of a woman."

Scarlet swallowed the emotions threatening to fall from her lips. She wanted to pull him into her arms, spend the day wrapped around him, and whisper all the reasons she loved him. That would be way more than their fragile reunion could probably handle.

"Let's start with coffee," she said squeezing his fingers in her own. It wasn't the best response, but it was a start. The rebirth of something old from something new.

Acknowledgments

There is a plethora of people I could thank in this section. Mostly, the Little Amps Coffee Roasters (as I mentioned in my dedication) for allowing me to take up space and drink away my problems while writing this book. Nanowrimo obviously because without which this novel would have never been written. Dave Cooper for brainstorming this idea with me. For my friends Mia and Kirsten for also brainstorming with me and supporting me in this endeavor.

Other obvious gratitude received would be my family. My mom and youngest sister specifically for helping me find the time to get the writing done. My various editors over the years who have helped me become better writers.

Finally, I owe so much to my cover artist, Victoria Miller, and my editor, Jen Bradlee. I would never have gotten this far without their support and guidance. You girls ROCK.

Revelations

The Four Horseman of the Apocalypse –

Cloris – Horsemen of Death

When the Lamb broke the fourth seal, I heard the voice of the fourth living creature saying, "Come and see." I looked, and behold, an ashen horse; and he who sat on it had the name Death; and Hades was following with him. Authority was given to them over a fourth of the earth, to kill with sword and with famine and with pestilence and by the wild beasts of the earth.

Katherine – Horsemen of Famine

When He broke the third seal, I heard the third living creature saying, "Come and see." I looked, and behold, a black horse; and he who sat on it had a pair of scales in his hand. And I heard something like a voice in the center of the four living creatures saying, "A quart of wheat for a denarius, and three quarts of barley for a denarius; and don't damage the oil and the wine."

Scarlet – Horsemen of War

When He broke the second seal, I heard the second living creature saying, "Come and see." And another, a red horse, went out; and to him who sat on it, it was granted to take peace from the earth, and that men would slay one another; and a great sword was given to him.

Bianca – Horsemen of Conquest

Then I saw when the Lamb broke one of the seven seals, and I heard one of the four living creatures saying as with a voice of thunder, "Come and see." I looked, and behold, a white horse, and he who sat on it had a bow; and a crown was given to him, and he went out conquering and to conquer.

Monica Corwin is an outspoken writer who attempts to make romance accessible to everyone no matter his or her preference. As a new Northern Ohioan, Monica enjoys snowdrifts, three seasons, and a dislike of the Michigan football program. When not writing Monica spends time with her daughter and her ever growing collection of Arthurian Legend tomes. She can be found on the web at www.monicacorwin.com or @monica_corwin on Twitter.

Made in the USA
Middletown, DE
05 November 2017